RAGGEDY ANN
IN THE
DEEP DEEP WOODS

RAGGEDY ANN
IN THE
DEEP DEEP WOODS

WRITTEN AND ILLUSTRATED
BY
Johnny Gruelle

SIMON & SCHUSTER BOOKS FOR YOUNG READERS

Ne~ ~apore

PUBLISHER'S NOTE:

Simon & Schuster Books for Young Readers is proud to be reissuing this
American classic in the format in which it was originally published. The color
illustrations have been reproduced from those in the early printings, thus
restoring the delicacy and detail that were lost as the plates deteriorated over
many printings. We have restored the endpapers and the jacket to their origi-
nal condition and, as in that edition, there is no table of contents. The book is
printed on acid-free paper for permanence and signature-sewn in the tradi-
tional manner for ease of use.

 SIMON & SCHUSTER BOOKS FOR YOUNG READERS
An imprint of Simon & Schuster Children's Publishing Division
1230 Avenue of the Americas, New York, New York 10020
Copyright 1930 by John B. Gruelle, Norwalk, Connecticut, USA
Copyright renewed 1951 by Myrtle Gruelle
First Simon & Schuster Books for Young Readers Edition 2002
All rights reserved, including the right of reproduction in whole or in part in any
form.
SIMON & SCHUSTER BOOKS FOR YOUNG READERS is a trademark of Simon &
Schuster. The names and depictions of Raggedy Ann and Raggedy Andy are trade-
marks of Simon & Schuster.

The text for this book is set in Caslon Old Face.
Printed in Hong Kong
10 9 8 7 6 5 4 3 2 1
Library of Congress Cataloging-in-Publication Data
Gruelle, Johnny, 1880-1938.
Raggedy Ann in the deep deep woods / written and illustrated by Johnny Gruelle.
p. cm.
Summary: Raggedy Ann and Andy spend a wonderful day with their woodland
friends, using their magical pebble to make everyone's dreams come true.
ISBN 0-689-84970-2
[1. Dolls—Fiction. 2. Wishes—Fiction.]
PZ7.G9324 Raek 2002
[E]—dc21
2001049222

TO

BETTY KERN ...

who hears the magical melodies
of Fairyland ~
this book is affectionately dedicated.

Johnny Gruelle
Norwalk ~ Connecticut,
September first ~ 1929

A WISHING PEBBLE PICNIC

RAGGEDY ANN and Raggedy Andy were sitting under a tree in the deep, deep woods, filled with fairies 'n' everything, drinking a glass of soda water through two straws. It was a very nice glass of soda water for it had come to them through a wish Raggedy Ann had made to find out if her Wishing Pebble was inside her rag body where she would not lose it. And I guess you know that a glass of magical soda water is better—if that is possible—than the best soda water you can ever buy in the stores.

And Raggedy Ann and Raggedy Andy were so happy, and they were so busy laughing and talking and enjoying the soda water that they did not know anyone was in back of them, until someone spoke in a very, very gruff voice, *"What are you doing there?"*

Raggedy Ann and Raggedy Andy both jumped to their feet so suddenly that they overturned the glass of soda water.

"Now see what you made us do!" Raggedy Ann said to the queer little creature standing laughing at them.

"Why! I didn't spill the glass of water," he said.

"I know you didn't!" said Raggedy Ann. "But it was impolite to speak so loud right in back of us when we did not even know you were there. And besides, it wasn't a glass of water. It was SODA WATER!"

"Was it good?" the queer little creature asked.

Raggedy Ann and Raggedy Andy looked at each other in surprise. "Is it possible that you have never, never tasted ice cream sodas, Mister, Mister What-ever-your-name-is?"

"My name is Skeezer," the queer little creature said, and then added, "No, I have never, never tasted ice cream soda water."

"Then you sit right there," said Raggedy Ann. "And, Raggedy Andy, you sit right here, and close your eyes, everybody, and count three, while I wish for us each to have a glass of ice cream soda water!"

"My! Isn't it cold!" exclaimed Skeezer as he felt the glass of ice cream soda water in his hands.

"Just you taste it," said Raggedy Andy. "Then you'll know how good it is."

"Is it really good?" a little voice behind Skeezer asked, and the Raggedys saw Scootie Squirrel coming down the tree.

"*Mmm*," Skeezer replied to Scootie Squirrel, "just you taste it, Scootie!"

"I'll wish for Scootie to have a glass, too," said Raggedy Ann. And then, as other little woodland creatures came up and looked at the glasses of soda water with longing in their bright little eyes, Raggedy Ann wished for a glass of soda water for each one of them, too.

There was Charlie Chipmunk, Mrs. Reta Rabbit and the two little Bunny-rabbit twins, and there was Wallace Woodpecker and Winnie Woodpecker and Pauline Porcupine, and Henry and Henrietta Hedgehog and a lot of little Cheepybirds. None of them had ever tasted ice cream soda water before, and they laughed and chattered and twittered with happiness while they ate it.

"It's just like a nice picnic!" cried Mrs. Reta Rabbit as she put bibs on the Bunny-rabbit twins so the strawberry sodas would not soil their pretty little bunnykin waists.

Raggedy Ann and Raggedy Andy laughed and had as much fun as anyone there, for, by giving happiness to everyone, they filled their little cotton stuffed bodies with something like a glow of warm sunshine and added to their own pleasure.

"Let's make it a real-for-sure, great, big, large picnic and invite all the creatures of the deep, deep woods," suggested Raggedy Andy.

So Charlie Chipmunk ran, and Wallie Woodpecker flew through the woods and invited everyone they met. In a very short time, there were hundreds of little woodland creatures sitting around Raggedy Ann and Raggedy Andy enjoying ice cream sodas. And when they had had all the soda water they wished, Raggedy Ann and Raggedy Andy let each one wish for something he wanted most and then Raggedy Ann and Raggedy Andy wished that each little woodland creature's wish would come true. So after the picnic, the deep, deep woods, filled with fairies 'n' everything rang with the songs and merry chatter of the happy little woodland creatures.

When the last little creature had run away with his present, Raggedy Ann and Raggedy Andy smiled into each other's shoe button eyes, but they never said a word. After giving so much happiness to others, it seemed to the Raggedys as if they were being held in a loving hug of dear Mother Nature, and this made them too happy to talk.

THE FAIRY RING

HOW pleasant it is to walk through the deep, deep woods and hear and see fairies 'n' everything all about you as you go. On every side the rippling melodies from the pretty birds greet your ears and beautiful flowers nod to you as you pass. Truly it is very, very pleasant. And so Raggedy Ann and Raggedy Andy found it as they wandered through the deep, deep woods, filled with fairies 'n' everything.

Little sparkling eyes peeped out at them from behind ferns and flowers and timid little woodland creatures scampered in front of them as they walked along. But Raggedy Ann and Raggedy Andy did not frighten any of the woodland creatures they met. No indeed! There is a certain magic in the deep, deep woods which tells each and every little creature when one who is kindly of heart passes. And when this whisper of magic says, "Do not be afraid, for this is a friendly heart!" the little woodland folk know that the magic whisper is true and whoever is passing is a friend.

If Raggedy Andy had had a candy heart like Raggedy Ann's, perhaps it would have felt just as warm with pleasure, but Raggedy Andy enjoyed the deep, deep woods just the same. And when one of the little woodsfolk came up and sniffed at Raggedy Andy's cotton stuffed legs, Raggedy Andy gave the little creature a soft, raggedy hug.

Raggedy Ann and Raggedy Andy stopped at a great big tree and watched beneath it, in the soft, velvety moss, a band of tiny little fairies playing. These were very tiny fairies, only three inches high, and they were as dainty in their pretty fairy dresses as the little pink and white flowers that peep from the grass in the early springtime.

Ten little fairies played there, and their tiny voices sounded as sweet, as they sang in their game, as the wind when it plays upon an Æolian harp. Raggedy Ann and Raggedy Andy, each with an arm over the other's shoulder, watched and were happy, their rag faces wrinkled in broad smiles and their shoe button eyes dancing with pleasure at the sight.

"How I should like to squeeze the dear little fairies!" the Raggedys both thought; but they knew this would spoil the fairies' game, so they remained silent and just watched.

The tiny, little fairies formed a circle and danced, their tiny slippers barely touching the soft velvety moss. As they sang faster, the tiny little fairies danced faster and whirled about so rapidly, the Raggedys could scarcely see them move their twinkling feet.

Soon the fairies rose in the air and danced in a fairy ring among the lower branches of the great tree, then floated again to the velvety moss below. When the dainty, tiny fairies had circled into the air ten times, they stayed upon the green mossy carpet, hand-in-hand, whirling in a circle, growing more airy as they danced, until Raggedy Ann and Raggedy Andy saw them only as a hazy white smoke in the shape of a ring.

Raggedy Ann and Raggedy Andy rubbed their rag

[11]

hands over their shoe button eyes as the ring of smoke disappeared and, with it, all signs of the tiny little fairies. But when the Raggedys walked out upon the velvety green moss where the fairies had been dancing a moment before, they saw, peeping up through the soft green moss, little buttons of white.

"Hmmm," mused Raggedy Andy, "they have lost the buttons off their dresses."

"All the buttons form a ring," said Raggedy Ann as she sat down and gently pushed the soft moss away from one of the buttons.

"Why! They are not buttons, Raggedy Andy!" cried Raggedy Ann. "They are tiny little mushrooms!"

Just then Skeezer walked up to the Raggedys. "Hello!" he said. "Have you been watching the fairies dance, Raggedy Ann and Raggedy Andy?"

Raggedy Ann and Raggedy Andy told Skeezer about the pretty, tiny little fairies.

"I have watched them many times," said Skeezer. "And after each dance, they leave the circle of mushrooms in the moss or in the grass, and everyone who finds this circle may know that the tiny, little fairies have been dancing in a fairy ring!"

"Oh, yes!" said Raggedy Ann. "I remember once we saw a ring like this on the lawn at home, and some of the older folks said, 'It's a fairy ring!'"

"Wasn't it nice that we could watch the fairies as they made the fairy ring?" said Raggedy Andy. And, indeed, Raggedy Ann thought it was a great treat.

FLYING WITH THE SQUIRRELS

"**H**ELLO, Charlie Chipmunk!" Raggedy Andy waved his hand to a little creature sitting on the limb of a tree in the deep, deep woods filled with fairies 'n' everything. "How are you today?"

"Oh, I am very, very well today!" the little creature replied. "But I am not Charlie Chipmunk, I am Fritzie Flying-squirrel."

"Are you joking?" Raggedy Ann asked him. "Squirrels cannot fly you know, unless some one carries them!"

"Ho, ho! Raggedy Ann, don't you believe it! I cannot fly like a Cheepybird, but I can glide in a great swoop from a high limb of one tree down to the trunk of another tree," said Fritzie Flying-squirrel.

"Do you really believe he can?" Raggedy Andy asked in a whisper of Raggedy Ann.

"Just you wait until I get the kernel out of this beech-nut, and I'll show you what a good scooter I am," Fritzie Flying-squirrel said, for he had heard Raggedy Andy's whisper.

"Your ears must be very sharp!" laughed Raggedy Ann.

[13]

"I can hear very well," replied Fritzie. "But now I have eaten the beechnut, so watch me." He ran nimbly to the trunk of the tree and up, up until he reached one of the top branches. Out on this he ran and gave a leap into the air.

"My, my!" said Raggedy Ann. "He'll get an awful bump when he strikes the ground. I am sorry we asked him to try it. Squirrels can't fly, that's certain!"

But Fritzie Flying-squirrel knew what he was doing; for he had done it time and time again. He spread all four little feet out sideways so that his little suit seemed as flat as a pan cake. And when he leaped from the high branch and shot down towards the ground, he curved his little squirrel body up; then, instead of dropping straight to the ground, he began to swoop in a curve, and when about ten feet from the ground, he rose into the air and lit, with a run, upon the trunk of another great tree.

"Whee, I never thought you could do it!" said Raggedy Ann. "That must be fun, Fritzie."

"It is fun," Fritzie replied. "You should try it, Raggedy Ann and Raggedy Andy."

Fritzie Flying-squirrel ran down the tree and sat upon Raggedy Ann's lap and when he was this close, the Raggedys could see why Fritzie could swoop so gracefully from one tree to another. Mother Nature had made Fritzie's clothes so that there was a connection from his front legs to his hind legs and this, when he spread his legs out flat, made a surface that held him up when he leaped from tree to tree.

"Oh, we could not do it," Raggedy Andy said, "for our clothes are different from yours!"

Raggedy Ann jumped up and down, for her little rag head had been very busy. "We can swoop with Fritzie Flying-squirrel!" she cried. "All we have to do is to wish that we could be able to do just as he does when he jumps from the high limbs, and we won't even have to wish to have wings!"

And as Raggedy Ann said this, she wished that she could climb the tree just as Fritzie Flying-squirrel did. Up the tree Raggedy Ann went, followed by Raggedy Andy and Fritzie Flying-squirrel.

Up, up they climbed until they reached the topmost branches, then the three ran out on the branch and gave great leaps into the air.

Raggedy Andy turned over and over as he came down, and lit with a thump upon the ground, but he jumped up laughing, for of course, being made of cloth and stuffed with nice white cotton, it did not hurt him in the least.

Raggedy Ann and Fritzie Flying-squirrel made graceful swoops and it was a lot of fun.

"You must wish that you will swoop, just like Fritzie," explained Raggedy Ann to Raggedy Andy. "It's just the way it feels when the elevator man lets the elevator go down real fast and sudden-like."

"Let's try it again!" cried Raggedy Andy, and this time he made great, graceful swoops with Fritzie Flying-squirrel and Raggedy Ann.

And as other flying squirrels heard the shouting and the laughter, they too came out and swooped with Raggedy Ann and Raggedy Andy. And every once in a while, when they grew tired of swooping from one tree to another, Raggedy Ann wished for red lemonade and cookies, so that they could eat while they were resting. And as the cookies were filled with nut kernels, the flying squirrels all said they had never had such a nice party.

THE HOOTIEOWL PARTY

GRAN'MA and Gran'pa Hootieowl lived in the large beech tree, in a great hollow place in the trunk of the tree. It was a very cozy place in which to live, for it was always nice and dry inside and there were two little knot holes through which Gran'ma and Gran'pa Hootieowl could sit and watch everything that happened in front of their tree-home.

When Gran'ma and Gran'pa Hootieowl saw the two Raggedys coming through the deep, deep woods, filled with fairies 'n' everything, Gran'ma said, "Hootie, who are these two coming through the deep, deep woods, filled with fairies 'n' everything?"

"Don't you know who they are, Gran'ma Hootieowl?" asked Gran'pa.

"No!" Gran'ma Hootieowl answered. "Who are they, Gran'pa Hootieowl?"

"That is Raggedy Ann and Raggedy Andy. I met them out in the great yellow meadow, beneath the blue, blue sky one evening. They are very, very nice rag dolls, and everyone loves them very, very much."

[17]

Then Gran'ma Hootieowl walked out on her front porch and called to Raggedy Ann and Raggedy Andy.

"Oh, Raggedy Ann and Raggedy Andy, won't you come up to our beech-tree home and visit with us? It looks like rain, and we are very cozy up here!"

"Thank you very, very much, Gran'ma Hootieowl!" said Raggedy Ann. "We shall be glad to come up into your beech-tree home and visit you and Gran'pa Hootieowl, for it is beginning to rain and we always get so soggy when we get wet." So Gran'pa Hootieowl dropped his little rope ladder and Raggedy Ann and Raggedy Andy were soon in the Hootieowl beech-tree home.

Gran'ma Hootieowl was a nice-looking old gran'ma owl. She wore a little skirt of flowered goods which puffed out all about her, and a waist of old-fashioned material. And on her head, Gran'ma Hootieowl wore the dearest little old poke bonnet. Gran'pa Hootieowl was a quaint little old-fashioned gran'pa owl. Gran'pa Hootieowl wore black slippers with silver buckles and yellow trousers. His coat was very old-fashioned too, and so was his tall yellow hat.

"We must have some tea, first thing of all!" said Gran'ma Hootieowl, when Raggedy Ann and Raggedy Andy had taken comfortable chairs.

"Which would you rather have with your tea, field-mice or June-bugs?" asked Gran'ma Hootieowl.

Raggedy Andy looked at Raggedy Ann and neither one knew exactly what to answer.

Finally Raggedy Ann said, "Gran'ma Hootieowl, we do not feel very hungry, so if you have some, we should prefer to have honey cakes with nice white icing, or dough-nuts with powdered sugar on them!"

This made Gran'ma Hootieowl look in bewilderment at Gran'pa Hootieowl.

"Dear me suz!" said Gran'ma Hootieowl. "I never even heard of those things."

Gran'pa Hootieowl could only scratch his head, for he did not know what to say.

"I'll tell you what we'll do, Gran'ma and Gran'pa Hootieowl," said Raggedy Ann. "It will be lots and lots of fun if we pretend that you two have come to see Raggedy Andy and me, and we will get the tea ready and fix everything. Now Gran'pa Hootieowl can smoke his pipe, and you can play on the organ and sing, while Raggedy Andy and I get the tea ready."

And that is what they did, for Gran'ma and Gran'pa Hootieowl had never played that way before, and they knew it would be lots of fun.

Raggedy Ann and Raggedy Andy went out into the Hootieowl kitchen, and Raggedy Ann whispered to Raggedy Andy, "Let's give Gran'ma and Gran'pa Hootieowl a surprise!"

"Yes, let's do!" said Raggedy Andy.

"We will wish for soda water! That's a great deal better than tea, don't you think?"

"Uh-huh!" agreed Raggedy Andy.

So Raggedy Ann wished for ice cream soda while Raggedy Andy wished for sandwiches and cookies and doughnuts and ladyfingers and cream puffs.

My! Weren't Gran'pa and Gran'ma Hootieowl surprised when they tasted the good things.

"We will never eat field-mice after this," laughed Gran'ma Hootieowl.

"But we will have to!" said Gran'pa Hootieowl, "for after Raggedy Ann and Raggedy Andy leave we won't be able to get such goodies."

"Oh, yes, you will, Gran'pa Hootieowl!" said Raggedy Ann. "Raggedy Andy and I have wished that you shall have a cupboard in your kitchen which will always be filled with everything we are eating. So, whenever you have company, you can always get whatever you want, without any trouble at all!"

Raggedy Ann and Raggedy Andy had a lot of fun visiting Gran'ma and Gran'pa Hootieowl, for they pretended that Gran'ma and Gran'pa Hootieowl had come to visit them instead of their visiting Gran'ma and Gran'pa in their beech-tree home.

Raggedy Ann had said, while she and Andy were wishing for a lot of cookies, and lady fingers, and doughnuts with powdered sugar on them, and cream puffs, "Now Gran'pa can smoke his pipe while Gran'ma Hootieowl plays on the organ and sings!"

But Gran'ma Hootieowl did not play on the organ and sing. 'Cause why? 'Cause the organ was only a picture of an organ which Gran'pa Hootieowl had found one day and he had pasted it to the wall in his beech-tree home. When Raggedy Ann saw that it was only a picture of an organ and not a real-for-sure organ, she laughed and made a wish all to herself.

So, when Gran'ma and Gran'pa Hootieowl had eaten all they wanted, and had drunk five glasses of ice cream soda water—which was the first they had ever tasted—there stood a nice, lovely, shiny, brand-new organ, just as the picture had shown. Only this was a real-for-sure organ, and could squeak out beautiful tunes for anyone that knew how to play it.

Raggedy Ann could play *Peter, Peter, Pumpkin Eater* with one hand, but it sounded rather squeaky. Then Gran'ma and Gran'pa Hootieowl tried to play a lovely, squeaky tune but they did not know how.

"I guess we haven't practised long enough!" said Gran'pa Hootieowl.

"We need some music to play from," said Raggedy Andy. "That's what we need! I shall wish for some."

But when the music came, they found that no one could understand what the little black specks on the lines meant.

Gran'ma Hootieowl tried to pick them off the music, for she could not see very well except at night.

"It's no use!" said Raggedy Ann. "I'll have to play *Peter, Peter, Pumpkin Eater* over and over!"

"It is a very nice tune anyway!" said Gran'ma Hootieowl. You see she had never heard a nice, lovely, shiny, squeaky organ before, so of course she did not know very much about pretty tunes.

"I tell you what, Raggedy Ann!" said Raggedy Andy after Raggedy Ann had played *Peter, Peter, Pumpkin Eater* over and over about sixty-'leven times, "let's wish for the organ to play itself. Then no one will have to work the pedals or anything, and we can just sit and listen."

Raggedy Ann jumped from the organ stool and gave Raggedy Andy a hug and a kiss. "That's just what we should have thought of at first!" she cried. "You wish for it, Raggedy Andy!"

So Raggedy Andy wished that the organ would play itself, and would play sixty-'leven different tunes whenever Gran'ma and Gran'pa pushed a little button at the side of the organ.

"Now!" said Raggedy Ann, her shoe button eyes twinkling, as much as shoe button eyes can twinkle. "Now, let's just sit and listen and listen!"

And so they did, until such a lot of the little woodland creatures came to hear the lovely, squeaky music that Gran'ma and Gran'pa Hootieowl had to serve them all with goodies to eat. And some of the tunes on the nice, shiny, brand-new, squeaky organ were so hippety-trippety, the little woodland creatures all got the wiggles in their little toes. And the only way they could get rid of the wiggles was to dance to the nice, lovely, squeaky, hippety-trippety tunes.

So you see, Raggedy Ann's and Raggedy Andy's visit to the Hootieowl's cozy beech-tree home turned out to be a party for all the woodland creatures who lived in that part of the deep, deep woods, filled with fairies 'n' everything.

THE FROWNINGEST FROWN

"OH, HOW good and pleasant it is for everyone to dwell together in love and friendship!" sang Raggedy Ann at the Hootieowl party.

Raggedy Ann was not quite in tune with the lovely, beautiful, squeaky tune the organ was playing, but that did not matter so very much. It was a nice song, even if Raggedy Ann did make it up right in her cotton stuffed head.

Some of the woodland creatures who were at Gran'ma and Gran'pa Hootieowl's party came just because the lovely tunes from the nice, brand-new, shiny organ called to them. And if the lovely, squeaky music had not called to them, they never, never would have ventured up to see Gran'ma and Gran'pa Hootieowl. But when Raggedy Andy had wished for the nice, shiny, brand new organ and had wished that it would play sixty-'leven different lovely, squeaky tunes, he wished in just a speck of magic which made each one forget that he sometimes nibbled the others.

And anyway, when the brand-new, shiny organ played the hippety-trippety tunes, and everyone got the wiggles in their toes and had to dance, Gran'ma Hootieowl danced with Gran'pa Field-mouse and never once thought of nibbling even a tiny bite.

Then Raggedy Ann and Raggedy Andy showed all the woodland creatures there how to play *Spin-the-plate* and *Button, Button, who's got the Button?* and lots of other nice games, so the deep deep woods, filled with fairies 'n' everything, rang with the woodland creatures' shouts and laughter.

Now all this noise woke old Missus Witchie Crosspatch who lived down at the bottom of the beech tree in which the Hootieowl home was built. When old Missus Witchie Crosspatch had rubbed her eyes, she hopped right up and knocked upon the wall of the tree.

"Here!" she cried in her peevishiest peevish voice. "You stop that racket, whoever you are! It's too bad when a person can't sleep in the daytime without being awakened. Stop that yelling this minute, or I'll come up there and 'tend to you."

Of course no one paid any attention to Missus Witchie Crosspatch because everyone was having too much fun and making too much noise to hear anything disagreeable. So when the fun did not stop, Missus Witchie Crosspatch hurried and dressed and wearing her frowningest frown she came climbing up the rope ladder to Gran'ma Hootieowl's home.

But when Missus Witchie Crosspatch reached the front porch of the Hootieowl's beech-tree home, her toes began to wiggle, for the nice, shiny, brand-new squeaky organ had just started to play the most hippety of the hippety-trippety tunes. So Missus Witchie Crosspatch ran right into the room and went hippety-trippety right along with everyone else; but her face was wrinkled in the same frowningest frown until Gran'pa Hootieowl caught hold of her hands and whirled her about so fast, they both fell down

[24]

and knocked the frowningest frown right off of Missus Witchie Crosspatch's nose.

And when Gran'pa Hootieowl saw what he had done, my! he was startled, for no one had ever seen Missus Witchie Crosspatch without her crosspatch frown. Gran'pa Hootieowl started to hunt for Missus Witchie's frowningest frown, but Missus Witchie Crosspatch laughed out loud. "Ha, Ha, Ha!" just like that, and she said, "Never mind, Gran'pa Hootieowl, don't waste time looking for it. Let's hippety-hop some more, for the lovely tune from the nice, brand-new, shiny, squeaky organ makes my toes wiggle."

So Gran'pa Hootieowl and Raggedy Andy took turns dancing with Missus Witchie Crosspatch and everyone laughed until they had to hold their sides.

Now when the frowningest frown dropped off Witchie Crosspatch's forehead it had rolled right over near the brand-new, shiny organ and no one saw it at all, for frowns can not be seen at all unless you wear them on your forehead. And so, when Charlie Chipmunk was dancing, and his feet slipped out from under him, he fell and bumped his forehead right where the frowningest frown was lying. And when Charlie Chipmunk jumped up, the frown was stuck to his forehead.

Charlie Chipmunk is always a happy little fellow, laughing and chattering all the time, so everyone was very, very much surprised when Charlie Chipmunk frowned at Gussie Greysquirrel. Even Gussie Greysquirrel was surprised, and Gussie Greysquirrel was having the very best fun just at that time, too.

Charlie Chipmunk frowned and frowned, and then— he bit Gussie Greysquirrel right on the heel. Gussie Greysquirrel squeaked. He squeaked so loud that his squeak sounded louder than the lovely squeaky tune the nice, shiny, brand-new organ was playing. And when Gran'pa Hootieowl said, "Charlie Chipmunk, aren't you ashamed of yourself?" Charlie Chipmunk, instead of hanging his head and

being ashamed, stamped his foot and said, "No, I'm not!" and started to bite Gran'pa Hootieowl just as he had bitten Gussie Greysquirrel.

"This will never do!" said Raggedy Ann, very severe-like. "You have nothing to be angry about, Charlie Chipmunk!"

Then—Charlie Chipmunk bit Raggedy Ann.

Of course it did not hurt Raggedy Ann as it had Gussie Greysquirrel, but it made Raggedy Ann feel very sad to think anyone should grow angry over nothing. So Raggedy Ann held Charlie Chipmunk tight while Raggedy Andy wiped the frowningest frown off his forehead. Then, of course, Charlie Chipmunk was as happy as he had ever been.

"You see," said Raggedy Ann to everybody as she took the frowningest frown and tore it to little tiny specks, "when you wear a frown, it takes the fun out of everything, for it is just like a pair of spectacles that makes everything look entirely different from what it really is. If you ever, ever feel a frown coming on your forehead, and do not have a hanky for wiping it off, just start to giggle hard, and old Mister Frown will slide right smack, dab, off, and won't come back again!"

Then Raggedy Ann and Gran'ma Hootieowl went to the cupboard which Raggedy Ann had wished into the Hootie-owl kitchen, and they brought out ice cream and cookies 'n' everything nice. And while everyone sat upon the floor crosslegged and ate, Raggedy Andy recited some lovely poetry: *Higgeldy-Piggeldy, My Black Hen,* and *This Little Pig Went to Market* and lots of other lovely verses. Well! everyone ate so much they had to unbutton the top buttons, and Missus Witchie forgot that she had promised to "come up and attend to everyone," and Charlie Chipmunk forgot he had ever frowned, and they both laughed and had as much fun as anyone there.

TWO SOFT BROWN EYES

"THE deep, deep woods filled with fairies 'n' everything is a wonderful place! The farther we walk into it, the more lovely things we see," said Raggedy Andy.

"Yes, indeed," Raggedy Ann replied. "Just watch over there, amongst those green, green ferns, Raggedy Andy, and see if you see anything."

Raggedy Andy looked, and looked so hard his little shoe button eyes almost pulled the threads loose. (Raggedy Ann's and Raggedy Andy's shoe button eyes are sewed with strong white thread—the kind Mother uses for sewing buttons on.)

Raggedy Andy saw just what Raggedy Ann had seen: two great, soft brown eyes looking out at them.

"May we come over and visit with you?" Raggedy Ann asked the owner of the two great, soft brown eyes. Raggedy Ann did not wish to startle anyone by walking up without speaking first.

"Yes, indeed, you may!" a gentle voice replied. So the Raggedys walked over to the ferns.

The owner of the two great, soft brown eyes was Mama Deer and there beside her were two of the dearest, wabbly-legged baby deer you could ever hope to see.

The baby deer were so very, very pretty, Raggedy Ann and Raggedy Andy could not keep from smoothing their spotted coats.

"Have you named the two babies yet, Mama Deer?" asked Raggedy Andy.

Mama Deer laughed a soft deer laugh. "Oh, yes!" she replied. "One's name is Danny Deer, and the other's name is Dorothy Deer!"

"What dear names!" laughed Raggedy Ann. "And will they grow up to be nice big deer like you, Mama Deer?"

"I hope so!" Mama Deer replied as she smoothed the baby deer's shiny sides where Raggedy Andy had mussed their coats. "But sometimes," said Mama Deer, "fierce, wicked creatures try to harm us, and that is why we have such strong slender legs. We can not fight them when they attack us, so we just run as hard as we can. And," laughed Mama Deer, "that is a great deal faster than any other creature in the deep, deep woods can run."

"Why do the baby deer have these pretty spots on their coats?" asked Raggedy Andy.

"I'll tell you, Raggedy Andy!" said Mama Deer. "When baby deer are little they are called fawns, and they are taught right from the beginning to remain perfectly quiet when I hide them and leave them for a while to hunt for something to eat. I always hide them in places where the sun shines through the leaves, and, when the sun shines through the leaves it makes spots upon whatever is underneath just like the pretty spots on my baby deer. And should any creature look at the place where I have hidden them, though the creature may be looking right at my babies, he thinks it is just the sun shining through the leaves

[29]

and making the spots. Baby fawns are taught never to move, even if they are frightened, for if they move, then the creature who is looking for them can easily see them."

"I'm going to make a wish for your two babies," said Raggedy Ann. "I'm going to wish that they will grow to be nice, big, lovely deer like you! And," continued Raggedy Ann, "that wish will come true, for sure, 'cause I have a magical Wishing Pebble right inside my cotton stuffed body!"

Mama Deer was so surprised to hear this, she could say nothing. So, after giving both of the fawns a nice Raggedy hug, Raggedy Ann and Raggedy Andy left Mama Deer and her babies, and with their arms about each other, they walked away through the deep, deep woods filled with fairies 'n' everything.

A FEAST FOR WOODPECKERS

RAGGEDY ANN and Raggedy Andy, walking through the deep, deep woods filled with fairies 'n' everything, stopped now and then to speak to one or another of the woodland creatures they chanced to meet, or stopped to touch gently some pretty flower growing by the path. And, as they were looking at a very lovely red flower, and admiring its pretty shape, they heard above them a sharp *rap-rap-rappity-tap*, as if someone were drumming with two sticks.

When the two Raggedys walked around the stump of the tree, they saw Wallie Woodpecker sitting up there tapping upon the hollow wood.

"Are you hunting for bugs, Wallie Woodpecker?" asked Raggedy Ann.

Wallie Woodpecker had his long claws hooked into the wood of the stump and was sitting back upon his short stubby tail. He wore a lovely red cap and gay striped coat.

Wallie Woodpecker turned his head to one side and looked down at the two Raggedys. "Listen!" he said.

Raggedy Ann and Raggedy Andy listened and away off through the deep, deep woods, filled with fairies 'n' everything, they heard the same sort of noise Wallie Woodpecker had made.

"Do you hear it?" asked Wallie Woodpecker. "That is William Woodpecker, my cousin, sending a reply to my message."

"Oh, I know," laughed Raggedy Andy. "You were telegraphing to each other."

"Yes, that was just what we were doing," Wallie Woodpecker said as he flew down beside the Raggedys. "I had sent William Woodpecker a message asking if he and Winnie Woodpecker could come over for dinner today."

"And what did William Woodpecker say?" asked Raggedy Ann.

"He said, 'I'll be right over just as soon as Winnie Woodpecker gets back from the Katydid grocery.'"

"Then I 'spect that'll be pretty soon," said Raggedy Ann.

"It won't take them long," laughed Wallie Woodpecker. "But I don't know what I shall give them for dinner."

"Hm!" said Raggedy Ann. "Maybe you should not have asked them to eat unless you had something to give them to eat, Wallie Woodpecker."

"I never thought of that," said Wallie Woodpecker, scratching his head, "I never thought of that at all."

"Then," said Raggedy Ann, "we must get something to eat for them right away."

"Yes, indeed," agreed Wallie Woodpecker. "I'll see if I can find some bugs and other nice things."

"Don't bother doing that," laughed Raggedy Ann. "Both Raggedy Andy and I can make our wishes come true, and here is a great big white mushroom which we can use for a table. We'll just wish for everything we want and have a lovely dinner."

"I've often wished for things," said Wallie Woodpecker. "But they never, never came true! How do you make your wishes come true, Raggedy Ann and Raggedy Andy?"

"You see," said Raggedy Ann, "Raggedy Andy has a Wishing Stick inside him and I have a Wishing Pebble inside me, and we just wish, and it comes true!"

"It must be nice to have all your wishes come true," laughed Wallie Woodpecker. "But I wouldn't care to swallow a pebble or a stick. They must be very uncomfortable!"

"They might be if we were not stuffed with nice clean soft cotton," laughed Raggedy Ann. "But here come William and Winnie Woodpecker, so I'll just wish for everything to be right upon the mushroom table, and all we will have to do will be to eat."

As soon as he had introduced William and Winnie Woodpecker to Raggedy Ann and Raggedy Andy, Raggedy Ann said, "Dinner's ready!" And indeed it was.

Wallie and William and Winnie Woodpecker had never tasted anything except bugs and things like that in their lives, so you can imagine just how pleased they were when they tasted such things as cookies with icing on them, lollypops and bread and butter and apple butter jam. My! They all ate and ate and ate until Wallie and William and Winnie Woodpecker said they could eat no more, and they looked so drowsy and sleepy Raggedy Ann said, "You three Woodpeckers had better take a nice nap, and I will wish that the mushroom table be filled with nice things when you waken."

And when the Woodpeckers had thanked them, the two Raggedys, with broad smiles upon their rag faces walked on down the cool path through the deep, deep woods filled with fairies 'n' everything, leaving the three Woodpeckers nodding at the mushroom table.

TEENY, WEENY ELF GIVES SOME DIRECTIONS

"SH," WHISPERED Raggedy Ann to Raggedy Andy as she peeped under a mushroom which grew from the bark of a tree in the deep, deep woods, filled with fairies 'n' everything. "Don't make a speck of noise, Raggedy Andy, there's a little teeny, weeny Elf asleep in a cobweb hammock."

"Isn't he cute," cried Raggedy Andy, so surprised to see the cunning little Elf he forgot to be real quiet.

"There now!" said Raggedy Ann, "you have wakened him!"

"Oh, yo-hum!" the tiny little Elf yawned, as he sat up in the cobweb hammock and stretched his little arms. "*Mmmy!* I must have been asleep a long, long time."

Then, seeing the two rag dolls standing and looking at him, each rag face with a broad smile painted upon it, the Elf said, "Hello, Raggedys, how are you?"

"We are fine," said Raggedy Ann and Raggedy Andy. "One could not help being happy wandering through this lovely deep, deep woods filled with fairies 'n' everything!"

"Yes, that is true!" laughed the teeny, weeny Elf as he crossed one little leg over the other. "With so much to see when strolling through the woods and with the music of the birds happy in their tree swings, I do not see how anyone can help but feel his whole soul filled with the sunshine of happiness. But do you know, Raggedy Ann and Raggedy Andy, there is a poor little old woman living in a little stone house back farther in the woods who is always very unhappy!"

"Dear me! how sad!" said Raggedy Ann. "What is the trouble with her, Eddie Elf?"

"Well, I'll tell you Raggedy Ann," Eddie Elf replied. "This poor old woman lives in the stone house all the time, and she never, never comes outside at all. She just sits there day in and day out, crying!"

"And don't you try to cheer her, Eddie Elf?" asked Raggedy Ann.

"Oh, yes," Eddie Elf replied. "I go to see her almost every day, but she cries so loudly when I go in, I can scarcely hear myself think. I never have found out why she cries so much!"

"Shall we go to see the poor little old woman?" Raggedy Ann asked Raggedy Andy. And, as Raggedy Andy thought

it would be a good thing to do, he and Raggedy Ann followed the directions given by little teeny, weeny Eddie Elf, and soon came to the little old woman's stone house.

It was a cunning little stone house, not so large as some dog houses you see in back yards, and it had cunning little doors and windows just large enough for that size of house.

Even Raggedy Ann and Raggedy Andy had to stoop when they went in the front door.

There sat the little old woman in a teeny rocking chair, crying as if her little heart would break.

"Why are you crying so hard, Granny?" asked Raggedy Ann as she wiped the little old woman's tears from her face. "Just see how red it has made your nose!"

"Your nose is red, too," replied the little old woman.

Raggedy Ann and Raggedy Andy laughed and told the little old woman that their noses were just painted on their rag faces with red paint.

Then the little old woman told them why she was crying. "When I was a little girl, I made some candy one day. It was very nice candy too, for I tasted a little teeny, weeny smidgin of it. The rest I planted in that flower pot over there on the window sill so that it would grow into a candy plant, but I have watered and watered it every morning and it has never grown into a candy plant with candy on it. That is why I am so sad."

Raggedy Ann wiggled one shoe button eye at Raggedy Andy and Raggedy Andy wiggled one shoe button eye at Raggedy Ann. That was as near as they could come to winking at each other.

Then Raggedy Ann walked over to the flower pot on the window sill and wished that a nice lollypop plant filled with pretty colored lollypops of all flavors would grow in the flower pot and in a few minutes there was a lovely lollypop plant filled with pretty lollypops of all flavors.

"Now," said Raggedy Ann, "you can stop crying and

have lots of fun, for as soon as you pick one lollypop another will grow in its place."

This made the little old woman very, very happy and she gave Raggedy Ann and Raggedy Andy a great hug apiece.

"Now, I can invite all my friends in to eat lollypops," she laughed. "And if you will wait a few minutes, I'll have my friends here and we shall have a party!"

But Raggedy Ann and Raggedy Andy wished to walk farther into the deep, deep woods, so they kissed the little old woman good-bye and walked down the path. And Raggedy Ann made a wish that the little old woman would find an ice cream soda water fountain in her living room when she returned from inviting her friends to the party, and Raggedy Andy wished that the little old woman would find a great bowl filled with cookies covered with candy icing.

But, happy as the little old woman was at the nice things given her, she was not one half so happy as Raggedy Ann and Raggedy Andy; for, when one has been kind to another, one's heart is filled with twice as much happiness as he has given away.

THE LITTLE DWARF TELLS A STORY

WHERE the sunlight streamed down through the foliage in the deep, deep woods, filled with fairies 'n' everything, it made ribbons of light like shiny slippery slides, and the rest of the deep, deep woods was filled with mysterious blue green shadows. The great trees moved their branches in the gentle breeze and the leaves whispered to each other.

Where one of the ribbons of sunlight came down into the blue green shadows, Raggedy Ann and Raggedy Andy came upon a little Dwarf, sitting cross-legged on a large toadstool.

This little fellow wore a queer suit and a tall pointed hat; and as he sat there, he puffed upon a long, curved-stemmed pipe.

When the two Raggedys walked up to him, he took the long stemmed pipe from his mouth and blew three rings into the air, then, without so much as a good morning, he said:

"And the King went out into the great forest that day hunting. And in some manner he became separated from those who had gone with him. And after wandering around for a long time, he finally reached the house of a Magician. This was a very wonderful Magician, although the King did not know him to be anything but a very ordinary poor man.

"'Do you know the way out of this forest, my good man?' the King asked.

"The Magician said that he would be glad to show the King the way out of the forest, but that first he would like to have him come to his house and have something to eat and drink.

"This pleased the King, for kings get hungry, just like little boys, and he went with the Magician.

"The Magician gave the King everything he wished to eat."

"Cookies?" asked Raggedy Andy.

"I guess so!" laughed the little Dwarf. "After eating, they went out upon the Magician's front porch and sat down to talk.

"And while they sat and talked, the King saw that the wild creatures came right up on the porch, and were not in the least afraid of the Magician. This seemed very strange to the King, for he had seen, when he saw them at all, the wild creatures running away from man. The King had always gone into the great forest to hunt the wild creatures.

"And the King asked the Magician, 'What sort of magic do you use to charm these wild creatures? They seem to recognize you as a friend, and are not the least afraid of your harming them.'

"The Magician laughed when he replied to the King. 'I do use a wonderful magic charm,' he said, 'the most wonderful charm in the world. And yet, it is such a simple charm that hundreds who know of it hardly think it worth using. But with this simple, wonderful charm, the most savage creatures can be tamed and the most timid creatures can be made to trust you. With it kingdoms can be conquered and slaves be made to grow into kings!'

" 'This cannot be a simple charm which will perform such wonderful things!' said the King.

" 'Oh, indeed it is so simple that any child may use it and perform the great things of which I have spoken!' said the Magician.

" 'Then,' said the King, 'teach me this wonderful charm and I will give you half my Kingdom!'

"The Magician laughed softly, then replied, 'This charm, oh, King, I have used with you, and you see that you have already promised me half your Kingdom; but I will tell you just what the wonderful charm is, and if you do not think it too simple, you can test it out for yourself!'

" 'What is it?' asked the King, excited at learning such a great secret. 'What is the wonderful charm?'

" 'It is the charm of being kind!' replied the Magician.

"And that's the end of the story," said the little Dwarf, as he puffed again on his long stemmed pipe.

Raggedy Ann and Raggedy Andy thought to themselves, "How true, and yet how simple! A wondrous charm within the reach of all."

And their little shoe button eyes caught the twinkle in the little dwarf's eyes, and their cotton stuffed bodies seemed to be filled with a glow of sunny happiness, for they knew and used the wonderful charm, the charm of being kind.

BENNY BUNNY

RAGGEDY ANN and Raggedy Andy were walking through the deep, deep woods, filled with fairies 'n' everything, when they were surprised to hear the whir of wings above their heads and to see Wallie Woodpecker flying down to them. Wallie Woodpecker was so excited he could scarcely speak, and Raggedy Ann and Raggedy Andy had to ask him to repeat what he said five times before they could understand.

"Come quickly, Raggedy Ann and Raggedy Andy. Little Benny Bunny is acting so funny, I am afraid something is wrong!"

"Where is Benny Bunny?" asked Raggedy Ann.

"He's right over that knoll there," Wallie Woodpecker replied. "He has a string fastened to him, and he is dancing around, and kicking up his heels, and turning somersaults."

"Maybe he is having fun doing all this," said Raggedy Andy.

"Oh, no!" Wallie Woodpecker replied, very excitedly. "He isn't doing it for fun. Please hurry, Raggedy Ann and Raggedy Andy."

"You fly ahead and show us where Benny Bunny is,

and we'll follow you, Wallie Woodpecker," said Raggedy Ann.

So Wallie Woodpecker pushed his little red cap down tight on his head and his wings whistled as he flew through the deep, deep woods. Raggedy Ann and Raggedy Andy ran after Wallie Woodpecker as fast as their little cotton-stuffed rag legs would carry them, until they came to where Benny Bunny was jumping and twisting and turning somersaults.

Raggedy Ann and Raggedy Andy ran up to Benny Bunny and held him still so that they could see what was the trouble with him. And what do you think? Benny Bunny had caught his head in a noose-trap while he was hopping along his own little path through the woods, and the noose had pulled tight around his neck. The other end of the string was fastened to a small bush and Benny Bunny pulled and pulled, and twisted and wiggled and turned somersaults, but he could not get loose.

Even while Raggedy Ann and Raggedy Andy held Benny Bunny, he kicked so hard, he almost knocked them over. But they held him tight until Raggedy Andy could untie the string and take it off Benny Bunny's neck.

"There!" said Raggedy Ann as Benny Bunny sat down and looked at them. "Now you do not need to twist and wiggle and kick and turn somersaults any more, Benny Bunny! You were caught in a trap, that's what it was."

"Whoever placed it there was very, very wicked," said Wallie Woodpecker. "If they had tied the string to a stout little tree and had bent the tree down, then Benny Bun-ny, you would not have wiggled and twisted very long, for the little tree would have sprung up and carried you into the air as soon as you touched the noose, and you would have just hung there!"

"I'm glad it wasn't tied to a stout little tree!" said Benny Bunny. "The noose alone, tied to the little bush, was bad enough."

Raggedy Ann and Raggedy Andy smoothed Benny Bunny's pretty little coat and Raggedy Ann tied his little neck tie, for he was all mussed from wiggling and kicking and turning somersaults.

Then Raggedy Andy went behind a tree and wished. He wished very hard, so hard that had he not had shoe button eyes, Raggedy Andy would have closed them. But, of course, he could not close his shoe button eyes. He wished very hard, just the same, so that when he came out from behind the tree, Raggedy Andy held a pretty little red basket in his hand and he gave it to Benny Bunny.

"Here, Benny Bunny," said Raggedy Andy. "Take this nice little red basket home just as fast as you can hop. It's a surprise for you and your Mamma and all the rest of the Bunny family. But do not stop to peep inside, or it will melt, and then the ice cream will all spill out."

"Oh, thank you so very, very much!" Benny Bunny said as he took the basket. "Mamma wanted some ice cream all day yesterday, and won't she be pleased to get this? Yes, indeed!"

And Benny Bunny, with the pretty little red basket, filled with magic ice cream ran down the path to his home lickety-split.

And Wallie Woodpecker looked so funny when he heard what was in the pretty little red basket, Raggedy Ann wished for Wallie Woodpecker to have one.

"For," said Raggedy Ann, "Wallie Woodpecker really was the one who saved Benny Bunny, and he should have a lot of ice cream, too."

And Wallie Woodpecker thanked the Raggedys and flew to his stump home, and as Raggedy Ann and Raggedy Andy walked on through the deep, deep woods, filled with fairies 'n' everything, they could hear Wallie Woodpecker sending his *rappy-tap* message asking all the other Woodpeckers to come and share his present.

QUEER KITTIES

RAGGEDY ANN and Raggedy Andy sat down beside Laughing Brook, which tinkled and giggled merrily as it dashed over the stones through the deep, deep woods, and as they sat there, just thinking and thinking how lovely everything was and neither saying a word, they heard kittens, crying.

"Dear me!" said kindly Raggedy Ann. "I wonder if a lot of dear little kittens have wandered into the deep, deep woods and are lost?"

"If they have, we must try and find some kind hearted little gnomes or fairies to give them nice comfortable homes!" said Raggedy Andy.

"Shall we walk through the bushes and see if we can find them?" Raggedy Ann asked.

"Oh, yes," Raggedy Andy replied. "The dear little kitties may try to walk on the grass where it bends over Laughing Brook, and they may fall into the water and get wet!"

Raggedy Ann arose and smoothed out her nice clean, white apron and helped Raggedy Andy to his feet. Then

the two kindly Raggedys walked through the high bushes toward where the kitties seemed to be.

But when they reached there, they found that the cries of the kitties came from a clump of pussy willow trees growing along the bank of Laughing Brook. And, as the two surprised rag dolls looked up into the pussy willow trees, the cries of the kitties ceased.

"I'll bet a nickel it was the pussy willow meowing," said Raggedy Andy.

"Do you really think so?" Raggedy Ann asked. "I did not know pussy willows made any noise!"

"Neither did I," said Raggedy Andy. "But it must have been the pussy willows, for the sound came directly from here."

Raggedy Ann and Raggedy Andy walked under the pussy willow trees and looked up.

"There isn't a branch in any of the trees large enough to hold a fat little kittie without bending way over," said Raggedy Ann. "Someone must be playing a joke on us, Raggedy Andy!"

Raggedy Andy seemed to think so, too, and he caught one of the pussy willow trees and shook it hard.

"Meow! Meow!" came the kittie's cry from the tree he had shaken. And looking closely, the two Raggedys saw little sharp eyes laughing down at them through the thick leaves.

Raggedy Andy turned and wiggled one of his shoe button eyes at Raggedy Ann, and Raggedy Ann wiggled one of her shoe button eyes at Raggedy Andy. Then they sat down beneath the pussy willow tree and laughed as hard as they could, for they both knew who it had been.

When they could stop laughing, Raggedy Ann called up into the pussy willow trees, "Come on down, Kitty Cat-bird, and whoever is with you. You played a funny joke on Andy and me that time."

And, because they knew they had been discovered,

Kitty Catbird and three of her friends flew down beside the two Raggedy dolls. There was Kitty Catbird, and Charlie Catbird, and Katrinka Catbird and they all pecked at Raggedy Ann's apron pocket.

So Raggedy Ann, knowing that the Catbirds were hunting for goodies, wished for a nice little Catbird table filled with everything nice, and sure enough, there stood the cute little Catbird table, and on it was everything a Catbird might wish to eat.

Then Raggedy Ann tied a clean leaf napkin around each Catbird's neck, and she and Raggedy Andy walked away beside the Laughing Brook.

"Didn't it sound just like kitties crying?" asked Raggedy Andy.

"Indeed it did!" laughed Raggedy Ann. "Maybe the Catbirds cry like kitties to frighten off other birds who might harm them."

"Maybe they do!" laughed Raggedy Andy. "The next time we see Kitty Catbird we must ask her, Raggedy Ann."

A SURPRISE FOR THE BUNNY FAMILY

RAGGEDY ANN and Raggedy Andy walked down the side of Laughing Brook, which ran through the deep, deep woods, filled with fairies 'n' everything, until they came to a rabbit burrow.

"I wonder if this is where Benny Bunny lives," Raggedy Ann said as she pointed to the front porch sticking out from below a large tree root. "It is so nice and clean, I am sure it is the Bunny home."

"We might knock upon the door and find out," suggested Raggedy Andy. "Maybe all the Bunnies are down stairs in the kitchen eating the lovely ice cream you gave to Benny Bunny."

"Oh, maybe they are," Raggedy Ann said as she walked to the Bunnies' front porch and knocked softly with her rag hand.

"I guess they are not at home, Raggedy Andy," said Raggedy Ann.

"Let's go around to their kitchen door, Raggedy Ann," suggested Raggedy Andy. "I 'spect maybe they are all there eating the lovely ice cream."

[49]

So Raggedy Ann and Raggedy Andy walked around the Bunnies' home to the kitchen door and there they stopped in astonishment, for when they looked inside, all the Bunny furniture was knocked this way and that, and there were broken dishes upon the floor.

"Dear me!" said Raggedy Ann. "I wonder what could have happened? Do you think the Bunnies could have been quarreling over the ice cream, Raggedy Andy?"

Raggedy Andy was saying, "I do not think so, Raggedy Ann, for the Bunnies never quarrel!" when he heard a little noise inside the Bunnies' kitchen.

It was a very little noise, like this, "Mmmm! Lick! Lick! Lick!"

"Hmmm!" mused Raggedy Ann. "What do you 'spect that is, Raggedy Andy?"

"I don't know," replied Raggedy Andy in a whisper. "But you wait out here, Raggedy Ann, and I'll soon find out!"

Raggedy Andy tiptoed softly into the Bunny kitchen, and there, hiding behind the door was Freddy Fox. He was licking his lips just as foxes do after they have had something very, very good to eat.

Raggedy Andy knew in a moment that Freddy Fox should not have been in the Bunnies' kitchen, so he caught Freddy's suspenders and held him.

"Come here, Raggedy Ann!" Raggedy Andy called. "Here is Freddy Fox in the Bunnies' kitchen, and I 'spect he's eaten all the Bunnies up, every smidgeon."

"My! My! Freddy Fox!" said Raggedy Ann. "Have you eaten every smidgeon of all the Bunny family? Don't answer me, for I can tell by the way you lick your lips, you have just finished eating them!"

Indeed, Freddy Fox looked guilty. He wiggled his big toe in a knot hole in the Bunnies' kitchen floor, and hung his head, and mumbled under his breath. "Honest Raggedy Ann, I ate only their ice cream."

[50]

"Well!" said Raggedy Ann, very much relieved. "But then that is bad enough! Where are the Bunnies, Freddy Fox? Just tell me that!"

"I don't know," Freddy Fox started crying. "They were eating ice cream when I came by, and when I walked into their kitchen they kicked over the furniture and went lickety-split into the dining room and out the front door. Then I ate all the ice cream, and was waiting behind the kitchen door for the Bunnies to come back so I could thank them!"

"Just you hold Freddy Fox until I call his Mamma!" said Raggedy Ann to Raggedy Andy, as she went out the door.

Mrs. Freda Fox was a very nice Mamma Fox. She was so sorry when Raggedy Ann told her what Freddy had done, that she took Mamma Bunny's pan-cake paddle, and was about to paddy-whack Freddy Fox when he started howling very loudly, "Oh! Ouch! My stomach hurts!"

Mamma Fox winked her bright little eye at the two Raggedys and said, "Uh-uh, Freddy Fox! Now you see, you have punished yourself. You not only took what did not belong to you, but you made a pig out of yourself, and now you are paying for it!"

Freddy Fox howled and howled until all the neighbors came to see what it was all about. Mamma Freda Fox had to take Freddy Fox home and give him some bitter medicine, so bitter it took all the ice cream taste away. And then Freddy Fox had to go to bed for the rest of the day for being so naughty.

By the time the Bunnies came home, Raggedy Ann had straightened up all the furniture and had wished for a lot more ice cream. All the neighbors were asked in, so, after all, the Bunnies had a nice time and they were happier than ever, for they shared their nice ice cream with all their friends. And when you share the good things of life with those about you, the good things of life always seem to be ever and ever so much better.

There were so many of the neighbors at the Bunny party Raggedy Ann and Raggedy Andy had to stand outside the Bunnies' kitchen door, and their little shoe button eyes twinkled as they listened to the friendly chatter while the Bunny family and all the neighbors ate the lovely ice cream Raggedy Ann had wished for them. And the little magical Wishing Pebble, which was tucked away safely in Raggedy Ann's soft cottony insides, went *plumpity-plump!* just as anyone's heart goes *plumpity-plump* after they have done something kindly for someone else. And Raggedy Andy's magical Wishing Stick, which was tucked away safely inside his nice, soft, white, cotton stuffing, went *thumpety-thump*, for Raggedy Andy felt as happy as Raggedy Ann.

"Let's give the Bunnies and all their neighbors a great s'prise party!" whispered Raggedy Andy as he pulled Raggedy Ann's apron and led her around the corner of the Bunnies' kitchen. "See that nice little pine tree?" Raggedy Andy asked, pointing to a nice little pine tree about six feet high.

Raggedy Ann laughed a soft little cottony laugh, for of course anyone could see the pretty little pine tree very easily, especially when someone pointed to it.

"Well!" said Raggedy Andy, laughing too. "Let's wish for presents to be hanging on the pretty little pine tree, so when we cry 'Merry Christmas' and run, all the Bunnies and their neighbors will come out here and find the lovely little pine tree covered with lovely presents."

"All right, Raggedy Andy," agreed Raggedy Ann. "It isn't anywhere near Christmas time, but we can have just as much fun as if it were!"

So while the Bunnies and their neighbors laughed and chattered and ate 'leventeen dishes of ice cream apiece, the two Raggedys stood beside the pretty little pine tree and wished and wished. And when they had wished for about sixteen minutes, the pretty little pine tree was covered with lovely presents for all the Bunny family and their neighbors. As soon as Raggedy Ann and Raggedy Andy saw that everyone had eaten all the ice cream they wished, Raggedy Andy went to the kitchen door and yelled as loud as a cotton stuffed rag doll can yell, "Merry Christmas!"

Then Raggedy Andy ran and hid with Raggedy Ann in the thick bushes and the two watched the Bunny family and all the neighbors come running out of the Bunny home.

They came out so fast some of them rolled over each other, but they hopped up without even starting to cry, and over to the pretty little pine tree they ran. My goodness! So much chattering and excited happiness!

And Raggedy Ann and Raggedy Andy, peeping from their hiding place in the thick bushes, had to hold their rag hands over their painted mouths to keep their own happiness from bubbling out and letting everyone know where they were hiding. And there the two Raggedys sat for a long time after the Bunnies' neighbors had taken their lovely presents home and the Bunnies had run over to Harry Hare's house to show him what they had received.

Yes, Raggedy Ann and Raggedy Andy sat there for a long, long time and never said a word, for each felt as happy inside as a dicky-bird does when he sings his sweetest melody. And Raggedy Ann, her cottony voice sort of catching in her throat, finally leaned over to Raggedy Andy and whispered, "Now we know why Santa Claus brings Christmas presents, Raggedy Andy."

And Raggedy Andy smiled back at Raggedy Ann and nodded his rag head, for if it brought them so much happiness to see the joy their presents had given the Bunny family and their neighbors, how much more happiness it must bring to Santa Claus when he feels the great, great happiness rainbow sent out to him on Christmas morning from the hearts of those he has visited.

And if you wish to feel a weeny speck of the Santa Claus happiness, just try being generous and you will soon know that the happiness rainbow is really and for-surely true, forming a happiness bow between loving hearts.

HURRYING A TURTLE

RAGGEDY ANN and Raggedy Andy were sitting upon a large brown stone in the deep, deep woods, filled with fairies 'n' everything listening to the birds singing merrily to each other, when something came scuffling slowly along in the leaves. Looking down from where they sat upon the large brown stone, Raggedy Ann and Raggedy Andy saw old Mister Unk Timothy Turtle walking slowly along.

Old Mister Unk Timothy Turtle shuffled along very awkwardly for even though it was summertime, old Mister Unk Timothy Turtle wore a heavy overcoat, and he had to walk around every stick and stone he came to very slowly.

"Where are you going, Mister Unk Timothy Turtle?" Raggedy Andy asked in a kindly raggedy tone. "You don't seem to care if you never get there!"

Old Mister Unk Timothy Turtle when he saw Raggedy Ann and Raggedy Andy sitting on the large brown stone smiling down at him, took off his specks and wiped them with his red bandanna hanky. Then he sat down upon a little brown stone and said, "I'm in a great hurry, my dears! A very great hurry!"

"Hmmm!" mused Raggedy Ann and Raggedy Andy both together as if they could scarcely believe it.

"Yes, indeed!" continued Old Mister Unk Timothy Turtle as he stuffed his pipe with dried leaves and started to puff away. "I am in great haste! Very great haste!"

"Why don't you run then?" asked Raggedy Andy.

Old Mister Unk Timothy Turtle took his pipe out of his mouth and looked at Raggedy Andy in amazement, then his mouth spread into a wide grin and he shook his pipe at Raggedy Andy.

"You are trying to tease me!" laughed old Mister Unk Timothy Turtle. "You know I was running just as hard as I could run. In fact I have never hurried so fast before in my life!"

"Indeed?" Raggedy Ann questioned.

"Why are you in such haste, Mister Unk Timothy Turtle?" Raggedy Andy wished to know as he wiggled one shoe button eye at Raggedy Ann.

"Well," old Mister Unk Timothy Turtle said as he knocked the ashes out of his pipe. "Terrance Terrapin just came over and told me that he and Theresa Terrapin had sixteen children, and I am running back to see them; and if I don't hurry I'll never get there!"

"Were they just hatched this morning?" asked Raggedy Andy.

"Lawsy, no!" old Mister Unk Timothy Turtle replied. "They were hatched last summer. It took Terrance Terrapin nine months, fast traveling, to get to my house to tell me all about it and that's why I am hurrying so. I want to get to Cousin Theresa's house before the sixteen children grow up!"

"Then," said Raggedy Ann and Raggedy Andy, "we will help you hurry, Mister Unk Timothy Turtle. We will pick you up and run part of the way through the woods.

Certainly that should save you about six weeks traveling!"

"That will be very kind of you," said old Mister Unk Timothy Turtle as he put his pipe in his overcoat pocket.

So Raggedy Ann caught hold of one of old Mister Unk Timothy Turtle's hands and Raggedy Andy caught hold of the other, and then they ran through the deep, deep woods, being careful not to bump old Mister Unk Timothy Turtle against any stone as they ran.

But they had only run about twenty feet when old Mister Unk Timothy Turtle cried, "Please stop!" The Raggedys stopped, and Old Mister Unk Timothy Turtle wiped his forehead with his red bandanna hanky and said, "My, you went so fast it made me dizzy! I believe I will run along by myself if you don't mind, but I thank you just the same. I'm not used to traveling so fast!"

"All right!" laughed Raggedy Ann and Raggedy Andy. "We hope you have a safe journey, Mister Unk Timothy Turtle!"

"Thank you!" old Mister Unk Timothy Turtle replied as he started shuffling slowly through the leaves.

"Well, well, well!" said Raggedy Ann, as she and Raggedy Andy walked on through the deep, deep woods. "How often we hear folks complaining because they *haven't time to do this or that*. If they would only consider old Mister Unk Timothy Turtle and how slowly he has to travel, even when he hurries as much as he can, they would soon discover how much more time they have, and that they could easily find time to do anything and everything that is worth doing!"

PICKLEDILLY'S FACE

"WHO do you suppose that is?" asked Raggedy Andy, as he and Raggedy Ann peeped out from behind some ferns at a strange little creature just half as tall as themselves.

"I do not know!" Raggedy Ann replied. "Suppose we ask him, Raggedy Andy!"

The strange little creature was dressed in brown clothes and his face and hands were as brown as his little suit.

When Raggedy Ann and Raggedy Andy stepped out from behind the ferns and said, "Good morning!" the strange little creature blinked his round eyes at them and said, "Good morning!" in return. But his face did not change expression, nor did he seem pleased nor displeased that the two Raggedys should speak to him.

"We are Raggedy Ann and Raggedy Andy!" said Raggedy Ann as she held out her hand to the strange little fellow.

"I'm Pickledilly!" the strange little creature answered without so much as a smile.

Raggedy Ann and Raggedy Andy, smiling cheerily and good-naturedly, stood looking at Pickledilly.

"Why don't you smile when you greet people?" Raggedy Ann asked him.

"I can't!" Pickledilly replied.

"Why not?" Raggedy Andy asked.

Tears rolled down Pickledilly's nose and splashed upon his little shoes. Raggedy Ann, very tender, and because she had a candy heart, wiped Pickledilly's eyes with her pocket-hanky. It was the nice clean pocket-hanky Raggedy Ann always carried in her pretty white apron pocket.

But what was Raggedy Ann's surprise when she had wiped the tears from Pickledilly's eyes to see that her nice clean white pocket-hanky was covered with mud, and that Pickledilly had two clean spots around his eyes. This made Pickledilly look as though he wore a pair of white specs and it seemed very funny for the rest of his face to be so brown.

"Why!" exclaimed Raggedy Andy, when he saw Raggedy Ann's soiled pocket-hanky. "His face is covered with dirt, and the wet, wet tears made his eyes muddy. And then you wiped the mud from his eyes with your nice, clean white pocket-hanky, Raggedy Ann!'

"Yes!" Raggedy Ann agreed. "That's just what happened, Raggedy Andy, but I'm glad I soiled my nice, clean, white pocket-hanky, if it will help Pickledilly."

Pickledillys' eyes twinkled, but still he did not smile.

"Do you know what?" asked Raggedy Ann as she dipped her pocket-hanky in the Laughing Brook. "I'm going to wash Pickledilly's face nice and clean!'

And with the wet pocket-hanky, Raggedy Ann washed Pickledilly's face nice and clean while Raggedy Andy washed Pickledilly's hands nice and clean. Pickledilly wiggled and squirmed and twisted and wriggled while he was being

[59]

washed, but the two Raggedys held him so tight that he could not get away until he was nice and clean.

"Why!" cried Raggedy Andy. "He's a cute little fellow when he is clean!"

"I thought he would be!" said Raggedy Ann.

Pickledilly smiled at the two Raggedys and said, "At first I didn't want you to wash my face and hands but you held me so tight I couldn't get away, but now I know that was just what I have needed for a long, long, long, longest time. You know, Raggedy Ann and Raggedy Andy, I always wiggled and twisted and squirmed and wriggled when my Mamma washed my face when I was a boy, and I never tried to keep my hands and face clean. And when I grew up, why my face got so dirty it dried up, and then I couldn't smile or laugh at all. That is why everyone calls me Pickledilly: because I always wore a sour-pickle look on my face!"

"How sad for you!" said Raggedy Ann. "Little fellows do not know what they are missing by having dirty faces. Why! No one cares to see dirty faces on little boys, and perhaps people who want to be friends with them if they only had clean pretty faces, pass them by and say, 'What an ugly little dirty-faced brat!'"

"Yes, sir!" agreed Pickledilly. "That is just what lots of people did call me: 'dirty-faced brat!'" And Pickledilly threw his arms around Raggedy Ann and Raggedy Andy and kissed them both upon their rag cheeks. "From now on I'm going to keep my face nice and clean so that everyone will like me!"

"That will be very, very nice!" said Raggedy Ann. "And I'll tell you another thing, too, and as it is not a secret you may tell it to anyone else you care to, Pickledilly. Keep your heart and mind just as nice and clean by thinking kindly thoughts and doing kindly deeds, and you will find that every person you meet will not only smile at you, but will love you along with the cheery greeting they give you!"

THE RESCUE OF COUSIN SCREECHYOWL

A S THEY were walking under a great beech tree, Raggedy Ann and Raggedy Andy heard their names called, "Yoo hoo! Raggedy Ann and Raggedy Andy! Yoo hoo!"

Looking up into the great beech tree, they saw the large yellow eyes of Gran'ma Hootieowl smiling down at them. "Where are you going, Raggedy Ann and Raggedy Andy?" Gran'ma Hootieowl asked.

"We are not going, Gran'ma Hootieowl!" Raggedy Andy replied. "We are just coming back!"

Gran'ma Hootieowl laughed a chuckly owl-laugh, *Cluck-cluck-chuckle*, and pushed her large spectacles back from her nose.

"I'm glad that you are not going, Raggedy Ann and Raggedy Andy," she said. "For if you are just coming back, then you will have time to come up and see what I have in my parlor?"

"We have lots of time, Gran'ma Hootieowl," Raggedy Andy replied, as he helped Raggedy Ann climb up the long ladder to the Hootieowl home.

Of course Raggedy Andy did not need to help Raggedy Ann climb up the ladder for she could climb as well as he could, but Raggedy Andy loved Raggedy Ann very, very much and it is always polite to help one you love, just as it is always polite to help anyone else.

"What have you in your cozy parlor?" Raggedy Ann asked, as she and Raggedy Andy shook Gran'ma Hootieowl's wing, how-de-do.

"Just you come in and see, Raggedy Ann and Raggedy Andy!" Gran'ma Hootieowl replied as she led the way into the Hootieowl parlor.

It was very dark in the Hootieowl parlor. Hootieowls can see much better in the dark than they can in the light, so Gran'ma Hootieowl always kept the curtains down unless she and Gran'pa Hootieowl had company.

"There now! What do you think of that?" Gran'ma Hootieowl asked as she raised the parlor curtains and showed a little Hootieowl crib.

"Why, my goodness! Gran'ma Hootieowl!" cried Raggedy Ann and Raggedy Andy in one breath. "You don't mean to say that you have a new Hootieowl baby?"

Cluck-cluck-chuckle, laughed Gran'ma Hootieowl, "No I didn't say that, Raggedy Ann and Raggedy Andy, for you see, while it is a new baby, it does not belong to Gran'pa Hootieowl and me!" And Gran'ma Hootieowl pulled back the fleecy covering of the Hootieowl crib and showed the Raggedys a cunning little owl baby.

"Gran'pa and I just borrowed him-like," said Gran'ma Hootieowl. "You see, it is Cousin Screechyowl's baby. When Cousin Screechyowl went away and did not come back again, Gran'pa heard little Screamie—that's the baby's name—crying, so he borrowed him to take care of!"

"Won't Cousin Screechyowl come back and want her Screamieowl?" asked Raggedy Ann.

Gran'ma Hootieowl brushed a tear from her eye. "I'm afraid not," she said. "I'm sure Freddy Fox must have caught Screechyowl."

"Then," said Raggedy Ann, "Raggedy Andy and I will run right over to Freddy Fox's house and bring Screechy back!"

And not waiting to climb down the ladder, the Raggedys jumped to the ground and ran toward Freddy Fox's house.

"We'll find her!" they cried.

Freddy Fox lived right near the fairies 'n' elves and gnomes 'n' sprites, but Freddy did not know when to behave himself. No, sir!

"Wasn't Freddy naughty to take Cousin Screechyowl away from her baby, Screamieowl?" Raggedy Ann asked Raggedy Andy as she knocked upon Freddy Fox's front door, *Tap, tap, tap*, with her soft rag hand.

"Yes, indeed, Raggedy Ann!" Raggedy Andy replied. "But Freddy Fox will never hear you knock if you use your soft hand, Raggedy Ann. I will take a stone and knock real hard, like this." And Raggedy Andy took a large stone and knocked real hard upon Freddy Fox's front door, *Thump! Thump! Thump!*

"I do not believe Freddy Fox is at home, Raggedy Andy!" said Raggedy Ann.

"Ha!" Raggedy Andy cried. "Indeed he isn't at home now, Raggedy Ann, for I just saw the tip end of his fuzzy tail as he slipped out of his back door and ran between the rocks."

"Hmmm!" mused Raggedy Ann. "Then if Freddy Fox slipped out the back door, perhaps he doesn't wish to see us. Maybe we had better come back some other time, Raggedy Andy!"

"No, sir, Raggedy Ann!" Raggedy Andy said. "The reason Freddy Fox slipped out his back door without asking us to come in is because he knows that he has been very naughty—that's what! So we must walk right in and see if Cousin Screechyowl is there!"

"But it isn't polite to walk into anyone's house, Raggedy Andy!" said Raggedy Ann.

"I know it isn't, Raggedy Ann," Raggedy Andy replied. "But when someone does such naughty things as Freddy Fox, then we must walk right in."

So Raggedy Andy walked right into Freddy Fox's front room, and Raggedy Ann followed him.

"There, you see, Raggedy Ann!" cried Raggedy Andy, as he ran to a box in the corner and opened it. Sure enough! there was poor Cousin Screechyowl lying in the box with her nice brown and white dress all torn and her bonnet down over one eye. When Raggedy Andy opened the box Cousin Screechyowl couldn't stand up, so the two Raggedys lifted her and carried her as fast as they could to Gran'ma Hootieowl's house in the great beech tree.

Gran'ma Hootieowl knew just what to do for poor Cousin Screechyowl to make her well again. Gran'ma Hootieowl gave her two glasses of strawberry soda water every five minutes for half an hour and then a lollypop. Of course this made Cousin Screechyowl very, very well and she sat right up and held little Screamieowl, her owl baby.

"My goodness, Raggedy Ann and Raggedy Andy, you came just in time!" said Cousin Screechyowl. "Freddy Fox was just starting to put the kettle on the stove to make Screechyowl soup!"

"I'd rather have ice cream soda than Screechyowl soup, wouldn't you, Raggedy Ann?" said Raggedy Andy.

And Gran'ma Hootieowl winked her two large yellow eyes at Raggedy Ann as she went to the Hootieowl cupboard and got soda water glasses. And because everyone was glad Cousin Screechyowl had returned to little baby Screamieowl, they each had 'leventeen ice cream sodas to celebrate.

WHO'S GOT THE BUTTONHOLE?

RAGGEDY ANN and Raggedy Andy were still visiting with Gran'ma Hootieowl when Gran'pa Hootieowl came home from work. Gran'pa Hootieowl was a night watchman at a button hole factory, so he always came home to sleep some more in the daytime.

Raggedy Andy scratched his rag head when he heard that Gran'pa Hootieowl worked at a button hole factory. "For," said Raggedy Andy, "who ever heard of a button hole factory? That's what I'd like to know."

"Why! Haven't you ever heard of a button hole factory, Raggedy Andy?" Gran'pa Hootieowl asked as he ate his dinner.

"No, sir, Gran'pa Hootieowl!" Raggedy Andy replied. "I never heard of a button hole factory before."

"Then I must take you to visit the factory some time," Gran'pa Hootieowl said, "for they make the loveliest holes you ever saw in your life."

And Gran'pa Hootieowl took a whole lot of button holes from his pocket and showed them to Ann and Andy.

"They throw away all the lop-sided ones. I often bring

them home so Gran'ma Hootieowl can put them in our clothes. The lopsided ones are plenty good enough for us, for we do not go out much in the daytime."

Raggedy Andy started to carry the lopsided button holes to the door to see in a better light, but he stubbed his toe on a rug and fell flat upon the floor. And of course he dropped every single lopsided button hole and they went rolling right out the door and spilled to the ground below just as naughty Freddy Fox, with a large stick, started climbing the ladder to try to catch the Hootieowls and Cousin Screechyowl.

There were so many lopsided button holes and they spattered over Freddy Fox so thick and fast he thought at first it must be hailstones. But, wherever a lopsided button hole stuck to Freddy Fox's clothes, why, of course, it made a hole. Soon there were so many holes in Freddy Fox's coat and vest and knee breeches, the wind just whistled in.

And, when Freddy Fox felt the wind whistle through the holes in his clothes, he jumped from the Hootieowls' ladder and ran home just as fast as he could scamper. And he did not want very much to go home for he knew when he reached there his mamma, Mrs. Freda Fox, would paddy whack him soundly for having so many holes in his brand new suit.

"I 'spect we'd better run over to Freddy Fox's house and tell his mamma what he has been up to," Raggedy Ann said.

When she and Raggedy Andy came to Freddy Fox's home they heard the loudest racket inside.

"I'll bet Mrs. Freda Fox, Freddy's mamma, is paddy-whacking him for getting holes in his new suit," Raggedy Ann said to Raggedy Andy.

After a moment Mamma Freda Fox came to the door with the pan-cake paddle in her hand. "Did you ever hear such a racket in your life, Raggedy Ann and Raggedy Andy?" Mamma Freda Fox asked.

"Maybe you have been paddy-whacking Freddy Fox!"

"How did you ever guess it?" Mamma Freda Fox asked.

"Because," said Raggedy Ann, "you still have the pancake paddle in your hand, and we could hear you paddy-whacking Freddy Fox and hear him squealing."

"Do you know what, Raggedy Ann and Raggedy Andy?" Mamma Freda Fox said. "Only yesterday I took Freddy down to the Hoolygooly store and bought him a nice new red suit, and a few moments ago, he came home with it chuck full of holes. So I paddy-whacked him with the pancake paddle and sent him to bed. I will have to sew up all the holes."

Then Raggedy Ann and Raggedy Andy told Mamma Freda Fox how Freddy happened to have the holes in his new suit.

"But they are not regular torn holes," Raggedy Ann said. "They are lopsided button holes, and if you will let me, I can take all the lopsided button holes out of Freddy's nice new red suit."

Mamma Freda Fox was very glad to hear this so she ran in the house and brought out Freddy Fox's nice new red suit and her sewing basket and Raggedy Ann took a little pair of snipping scissors and cut all the lopsided button holes out of Freddy Fox's new suit.

"There!" said Raggedy Ann when she had finished. "It is as good as new! And here are all the button holes which you can sew on other clothes when you make them!"

Mamma Freda Fox laughed and thanked Raggedy Ann. "I had just rolled out a lot of dough when Freddy came home," she said, "so instead of using the lopsided button holes to sew on his clothes, I believe I will use the button holes to make the holes in my doughnuts!"

And this is what she did. And when the doughnuts were cooked, Mamma Freda Fox gave some to Raggedy Ann and Andy. And, of course, doughnuts are much better with lopsided holes in them.

RAGGEDY ANDY GETS CAUGHT

I GUESS you have been out in the deep, deep woods, filled with fairies 'n' everything lots of times. And if you have, then you know just how lovely every thing is there. The great trees above your head whisper as you pass beneath, "There is a nice little boy!" or "There is a nice little girl!" whichever you happen to be. And perhaps one whispering tree will say to another, "Don't you wish that nice little boy—or girl—could see all the fairies 'n' everything," and the next tree will rustle its leaves and whisper back, "It would be nice! Oh, yes, indeed!" And although you hear the trees whisper to each other, maybe you can not understand just what it is they say.

But with Raggedy Ann and Raggedy Andy it is different, for they know just what the trees are whispering about. They know just what the lovely birds are singing, and why the pretty little flowers nod their heads to each other. And it is because the deep, deep woods are so beautiful they know everything in it must be happy. That is why, when you walk through the deep, deep woods, you feel so happy, and why you laugh and shout and love everything you see. It is only once in a while that someone comes through the deep, deep woods who is himself selfish, and, of course, that person does not feel the joy and happiness about him.

Once, when Raggedy Ann and Raggedy Andy were walking through the deep, deep woods, suddenly they heard Jasper Jay high up in a tree scolding at someone down below; and Charlie Chipmunk, too, was chattering in angry tones at someone down below. Raggedy Ann and Raggedy Andy walked on tiptoes and peeped through the bushes.

There they saw old Mister Meany fixing something down in the grass at the side of the Laughing Brook, and Charlie Chipmunk and Jasper Jay chattered and fussed at Mister Meany until he had finished what he was doing and went away. Even then Jasper Jay flew after Mister Meany to scold him, but Charlie Chipmunk came down and walked beside Raggedy Ann and Raggedy Andy who wanted to see what Mister Meany had been doing.

Clack! something snapped right where Raggedy Andy stepped, and before he could say, "My!" two steel clamps jumped up and caught Raggedy Andy right where his blue pants buttoned to his striped waist. Luckily Raggedy Andy is made of cloth and stuffed with cotton, or the clamps would have knocked the wind out of him. It was bad enough as it was, for the clamps squeezed so tight Raggedy Andy's cotton stuffed stomach was only a quarter of an inch thick.

"Hmmm!" Raggedy Andy said, very much surprised.

"Oh, dear!" Charlie Chipmunk said. "Now you are caught in old Mister Meany's trap, and he will take you home as he does the animals he catches and sell your clothes!"

Raggedy Andy pushed upon the clamps of the trap and so did Raggedy Ann and Charlie Chipmunk, but they could not budge them one speck. And if Nester Gnome had not heard them talking and come to the rescue, there is no telling how long Raggedy Andy would have had to stay in the trap. But Nester Gnome's hands are very strong, even though he is no larger than Raggedy Andy. As soon as Nester

Gnome had rescued Raggedy Andy from Mister Meany's steel trap, they carried the trap and hid it where Mister Meany would never, never find it. When Raggedy Ann and Nester Gnome had patted Raggedy Andy's stomach until it was nice and round again, Nester Gnome gave each one of them a lemon lollypop, for lollypops are very good to eat after being caught in a trap, or at any time for that matter.

"Jasper Jay is a brave little fellow," Raggedy Ann said to Raggedy Andy as the two walked through the woods. "All the time Mister Meany was fixing his cruel trap beside Laughing Brook, Jasper Jay was quarreling and scolding him, and every other bird, and every creature in the woods knew when they heard Jasper Jay scolding that some 'meany' person was in the deep, deep woods."

"I am glad Mister Meany's trap caught me instead of one of the wood creatures," said Raggedy Andy. "It did not hurt me one speck to have the steel clamps snap tight against my stomach, but it would have hurt any wood creature."

"Listen!" said Raggedy Ann. "Jasper Jay is still scolding old Mister Meany."

And, indeed, when the two Raggedys came to old Mister Meany's house they saw Mister Meany asleep on a bench in front of his house, while above him in a tree, Jasper Jay scolded and fussed at Mister Meany in loud, angry jay-bird talk.

"You ought to be ashamed of yourself, old Mister Meany," Jasper Jay cried. "It is wrong for you to catch the woodland creatures in the cruel trap and sell their clothes!"

But old Mister Meany was sound asleep and he paid no attention to Jasper Jay's scolding.

And when Raggedy Andy saw one of old Mister Meany's traps lying beside the bench with its steel clamps wide open, without saying a word to Raggedy Ann, Raggedy

Andy ran and picked up the trap and poked it right at old Mister Meany's shoe. *Clack* snapped the trap, as it fastened its steel clamps around old Mister Meany's foot.

"Why, Raggedy Andy!" Raggedy Ann cried in surprise as Mister Meany awakened with a loud howl and danced about with the trap over his toes.

"*WOW!* That hurts!" old Mister Meany cried.

"Of course it does!" Raggedy Andy said. "And now you know just how it feels when the little woodland creatures get caught in the wicked, cruel traps."

Old Mister Meany took the trap from his foot and sat down upon the bench. "I never thought it hurt that much!" he said.

"That's just it!" Raggedy Andy replied. "People who are mean to little creatures never stop to think of the unhappiness they cause. But little creatures can be just as unhappy as large creatures if wicked people hurt them. When you take a little woodland creature away from its family and friends, you cause as much unhappiness as you would if you did the same thing to a person."

Old Mister Meany rubbed his aching foot with one hand and his head with the other for a while, then he got up, and taking his axe, he smashed every one of the cruel steel traps.

"There!" he said. "I have broken all except the one down by Laughing Brook and I will run right down there and break that."

"We hid it!" Raggedy Andy told Mister Meany.

"My foot hurts very much!" Mister Meany said. "But I want to thank you anyway, Raggedy Andy, for after this, I shall try to make up with kindness for all the unhappiness I have caused the woodland creatures!"

And that is just what Mr. Meany did, so that soon the little woodland creatures came to love and trust him. There is a whispering magic in the deep, deep woods which tells the little creatures who are their friends, and they are as happy in their wonderful friendships as we are in ours.

THE EIGHTEENTH STORY

BEARS—AND BEES—AND BUNNIES

"ISN'T this Mrs. Benjamin Bear's house, Raggedy Ann?" Raggedy Andy asked as the two Raggedys walking through the deep, deep woods, came upon a cunning little house nestling amongst the bushes and flowers.

"I believe it is, Raggedy Andy!" Raggedy Ann replied. "Let us go up the pretty little path and knock at the door!"

When the two Raggedys drew nearer the cunning little house, they saw that all the little windows were hung with pretty white curtains and the front steps were swept nice and clean.

"Mrs. Benjamin Bear is a nice housekeeper," Raggedy Ann said as she lifted the knocker and rapped, *Clack, Clack, Clack.*

"Well! Bless my old Bear heart!" Mrs. Benjamin Bear exclaimed when she came to the door. "It is Raggedy Ann and Raggedy Andy. I'm so glad to see you. Come in and tell me all about your adventures since I saw you a long, long time ago."

So Raggedy Ann and Raggedy Andy walked into Mrs. Benjamin Bear's parlor and sat down in comfortable rockers while they told Mrs. Benjamin Bear all their adventures.

"You would have had a lot of fun if you could have been with us, Mrs. Benjamin Bear," said Raggedy Ann. "We met a Dragon, didn't we, Raggedy Andy?"

"A Dragon!" Mrs. Benjamin Bear said in surprise. "My! Didn't he eat you up?"

Raggedy Ann and Raggedy Andy laughed at this. "Oh, no, Mrs. Benjamin Bear!" Raggedy Andy laughed. "If he had eaten us up we wouldn't be here now."

"Of course not," Mrs. Benjamin Bear laughed. "But I always thought Dragons ate people up."

"Don't you believe it any more, Mrs. Benjamin Bear," exclaimed Raggedy Ann. "Anyway, this Dragon was a paper Dragon and very, very nice," added Raggedy Andy.

Mrs. Benjamin Bear was going to ask something else about the Dragon when, outside the Bear house, a loud noise interrupted her, and up the path, racing as fast as he could come, was Buster Bear, Mrs. Benjamin Bear's little boy - bear. Mrs. Benjamin Bear opened the door and Buster Bear came bouncing in, howling as loud as a little cubby bear can howl. And behind little Buster Bear came ever so many bees, and the bees were buzzing loudly, too. Mrs. Benjamin Bear shooed the bees

out of the house and looked at Buster. Buster Bear's nose was swollen and he had big lumps all over his face.

"I wasn't doing anything," Buster Bear cried. "And the old bees came out of their house and sat upon my nose, and their feet were so hot they made my nose burn!"

"Where was the bee house?" asked Mrs. Benjamin Bear.

" 'Way up in a tree," Buster replied. "And I didn't do anything to them, and that's what they did to me!"

"Ha!" Mrs. Benjamin Bear said. "I see honey upon your chin, Buster Bear, so I know just what you did to the bees! You got into their honey, that's what! You took their honey; that is why the bees' feet were so hot. And because you told me a story, now you will have to go to bed!"

Mrs. Benjamin Bear put baking soda on Buster's nose to stop the pain, but he did not get any ginger cookies when Mrs. Bear and the Raggedys had their tea. And he made up his mind right then that he would never again tell his mama anything but the truth.

Raggedy Ann and Raggedy Andy liked Mrs. Benjamin Bear's ginger cookies and tea, for it was sassafrass tea. It was pink sassafrass tea and very, very good.

The ginger cookies were good, too, almost better than the tea.

Mrs. Benjamin Bear might have made little Buster Bear stay in bed all day if the Raggedys had not jumped up and run to the window to see what was going on outside.

And they saw such a pretty sight, Mrs. Benjamin Bear called Buster Bear to look, too.

"It's the parade of the Easter Bunnies," Mrs. Benjamin Bear told the Raggedys. "Every year just at this time the Easter bunnies all march to the Fairy Castle and get their magic paints for painting Easter eggs."

The Easter Bunnies were all white with pink noses,

and there were so many Raggedy Ann could not count them. (Raggedy Ann could count to ten easily, but after that she got mixed and skipped number thirteen and fifteen.)

Buster Bear forgot all about the bees and their hot feet when he saw the parade of the Easter Bunnies.

"Why are they all white, Mama?" he asked.

"Well, I will tell you just what Granpy Hoppytoad told me," Mrs. Benjamin Bear said.

"Once the Easter Bunnies were just like other bunnies, and when they colored the Easter eggs, why! they were just covered with red and blue and green and purple and every other color.

"And when they had finished coloring the Easter eggs, all the Easter Bunnies looked like crazy quilts. Now the Fairy Queen knew this would never, never do, so she sent for all the Easter Bunnies and said, 'Can't you be more careful when you color Easter Eggs?'

"The Easter Bunnies all told the Fairy Queen that they tried to be careful. 'Then,' said the Fairy Queen, 'If you cannot be careful, I shall have to make the colors careful, and see if we can keep the colors from getting on you instead of your getting covered with the colors!' So the Fairy Queen waved her magic wand and said, 'Hokus Pokus,' and all the fur of the Easter Bunnies was clean, and as white as snow; and the magic colors made by the fairies never spot the pretty white Easter Bunnies any more."

The Raggedys and Mrs. Benjamin Bear and Buster Bear watched the pretty Easter Bunnies until they were out of sight, and because Buster Bear had not had any ginger cookies and sassafrass tea before, Mrs. Benjamin Bear gave him some. Then she and Raggedy Ann and Raggedy Andy ate some more, too, because sassafrass tea is good for anyone in the Spring and ginger cookies are good all the year round.

DOCTOR LEWELLEN STORK

RAGGEDY ANN and Raggedy Andy were sitting under a clump of laurel bushes in the deep, deep woods, filled with fairies 'n' everything, listening to the whispering of the great trees above them, when who should come walking along but old Doctor Lewellen Stork.

"Now what in the world is kind old Doctor Lewellen Stork doing, walking along in the deep, deep woods filled with fairies 'n' everything, Raggedy Ann?" Raggedy Andy whispered in his quietest Raggedy whisper.

"Dear me!" Raggedy Ann whispered in reply. "I wonder too! Kind old Doctor Lewellen Stork very, very seldom walks any place except in the puddles along the misty, moisty marsh, or in the trickles of the tinkling Laughing Brook. Maybe he has lost his spectacles!"

"'Deed, he hasn't lost his spectacles, Raggedy Ann!" Raggedy Andy said. "Kind old Doctor Lewellen Stork has his spectacles right on his nose—I mean his long bill."

"So he has!" Raggedy Ann replied. "Then kind, old Doctor Lewellen Stork has lost something, I'll bet a million dollars."

"I believe he has," Raggedy Andy replied. " 'Cause, see? He's poking around in almost every clump of bushes and every hollow tree. I wonder what he is doing?"

"And I wonder, too!" said Raggedy Ann as she got upon her wobbly rag legs and smoothed the wrinkles out of her pretty apron. "Let's follow kind old Doctor Lewellen Stork and maybe we can see what he is hunting for, or maybe we can help him find it."

This pleased Raggedy Andy for he had wanted to do this as soon as he saw Doctor Lewellen Stork looking for something. So the two Raggedys took hold of hands and ran down the path until they caught up with the kind, old Doctor Lewellen Stork.

"If you tell us what you are hunting for, kind old Doctor Lewellen Stork, Raggedy Andy and I will help you hunt for it. We can find things very well, for we both have shoe button eyes," said Raggedy Ann.

Kind old Doctor Lewellen Stork chuckled softly and arranged his spectacles nearer his eyes.

"I'm looking for presents, Raggedy Ann and Raggedy Andy!" he said.

"Birthday presents, kind old Doctor Lewellen Stork! ' Raggedy Andy asked.

"You guessed it the first 'pop'!" Kind old Doctor Lewellen Stork laughed. "Ah!" he said, as he poked his long bill under a bush, "here's the first one I have found today."

And then——out of the bushes, he pulled, but ever so gently, the weeniest, teeniest little baby chipmunk. Kind, old Doctor Lewellen Stork put the weeny baby chipmunk in a basket lined with the softest, fluffiest down.

"But that isn't a birthday present!" Raggedy Andy said.

"Oh, indeed it is!" Doctor Lewellen Stork replied. "The fairies put the dear little creatures around in the deep, deep woods, and when I take them to some nice new mama and daddy creature, don't you see, that makes them a birthday present? First I must find three more little weeny, teeny baby chipmunks, then I will take them to Mr. and Mrs. Charlie Chipmunk!"

And because they had shoe button eyes, the Raggedys helped kind, old Doctor Lewellen Stork until he found three more baby chipmunks to take as a birthday present to the Charlie Chipmunk home.

Raggedy Ann and Raggedy Andy did not go with kind, old Doctor Lewellen Stork when he took the birthday presents to Mr. and Mrs. Charlie Chipmunk's home. 'Cause why? 'Cause when Raggedy Ann and Raggedy Andy had helped him find the little weeny, teeny baby chipmunks which had been hidden by the fairies in the coziest places amongst the flowers in the deep, deep woods, kind old Doctor Lewellen Stork had placed all the baby chipmunks in a basket lined with the fluffiest down and had flown away. And because the Raggedys could not fly along with kind, old Doctor Lewellen Stork, they had to run.

"Won't Mr. and Mrs. Charlie Chipmunk be s'prised when they see the cunning little weeny, teeny baby chipmunks kind, old Doctor Lewellen Stork has brought them?" laughed Raggedy Ann.

"Indeed, they will!" Raggedy Andy replied. "Let's hurry until we come to the chipmunk home, Raggedy Ann!"

So the two Raggedys caught hold of each other's rag hand and raced through the deep, deep woods filled with fairies 'n' everything.

And as they ran along, little woodland creatures peeped out from beneath bushes and from their tree home windows, and asked, "Where are you running, Raggedy Ann and Raggedy Andy?"

"Come along and you will see," the Raggedys replied. "It's a s'prise!"

So along behind the Raggedys the other little woodland

[83]

creatures ran, and this made a long string of woodland creatures running as hard as they could to find out what Raggedy Ann and Raggedy Andy were running to see.

And when Raggedy Ann and Raggedy Andy, followed by all the little woodland creatures reached the tree home of Charlie Chipmunk, there sat Charlie Chipmunk on his front step, smoking his little acorn pipe and smiling such a happy smile he could hardly hold the acorn pipe in his mouth.

Raggedy Ann and Raggedy Andy pretended they did not know Charlie Chipmunk's secret and they asked, "Why are you smiling such a happy, grinny smile, Charlie Chipmunk?"

"Just you come inside and see what kind, old Doctor Lewellen Stork just left Mrs. Charlie Chipmunk and me! I'll bet you will smile, too."

So Charlie Chipmunk put his pipe on the front step and took the Raggedys and the little woodland creatures into his house to see the cunning little weeny, teeny baby chipmunks.

"And," laughed Charlie Chipmunk, "Mama Chipmunk and I are just the happiest chipmunks in the whole deep, deep woods for kind old Doctor Lewellen Stork told us the baby weeny, teeny chipmunks were the cunningest ones he could find!"

And Mrs. Charlie Chipmunk laughed and said she thought so, too, and Raggedy Ann and Raggedy Andy hugged each one of the baby chipmunks and said *they* thought so, too, and all the woodland creatures said they thought the teeny, weeny baby chipmunks looked just like their Mama and Daddy.

Then, because the chipmunk home could not hold all

the woodland neighbors who came to see the new weeny baby chipmunks, Charlie Chipmunk and Raggedy Andy carried the cradles out to the soft grass in the front yard. And Raggedy Ann and some of the woodland lady creatures helped Mama Chipmunk get the loveliest lunch, so that all the woodland creatures could have a happiness picnic and share in the chipmunks' joy.

Raggedy Ann and Raggedy Andy were as happy over the little weeny, teeny baby chipmunks as Mama and Daddy Chipmunk and the other woodland creatures. And while they all sat around in the soft grass in front of the Charlie Chipmunk home and had a happiness picnic lunch, the Raggedys told all the woodland creatures how they had helped kind, old Doctor Lewellen Stork find the weeny, teeny baby chipmunks.

"You know," Raggedy Ann told the woodland creatures, "the fairies take the little weeny, teeny baby creatures and put them in nice cozy places amongst the lovely flowers, and when kind old Doctor Lewellen Stork comes along and looks for them, he finds them. Why, Raggedy Andy and I helped kind, old Doctor Lewellen Stork hunt for the new little babies, and we each found one, didn't we, Raggedy Andy?"

"Yes, that is true!" Raggedy Andy replied. "We each found a little, weeny, teeny, baby chipmunk."

"And you say the cunning little weeny, teeny baby woodland creatures are hidden amongst the flowers in nice, cozy places?" some of the woodland creatures asked Raggedy Ann.

"Yes, indeed!" Raggedy Ann and Raggedy Andy both replied. "And we did not have to hunt very long, did we?" they both asked each other.

When they heard this all the woodland creatures at the chipmunks' happiness picnic jumped up and cried, "We will hunt for the little weeny, teeny baby creatures underneath the flowers, too!" and away they ran in all directions.

[85]

Raggedy Ann and Raggedy Andy gave each of the cunning little baby chipmunks a soft Raggedy hug and ran after the woodland creatures.

"We will help you find the cunning little weeny, teeny baby creatures," they laughed, "for we have shoe button eyes and can see ever so well!"

So the woodland creatures hunted and hunted and the Raggedys hunted and hunted and they peeped into the coziest places amongst the flowers, but hunt as hard as they could neither the Raggedys nor any of the woodland creatures could find a single teeny, weeny woodland baby.

"Do you know what?" Raggedy Andy finally said to the woodland creatures. "The reason we can not find the little weeny, teeny baby woodland creatures is because we haven't spectacles like kind old Doctor Lewellen Stork. That's why!"

"But!" all the woodland creatures cried. "Both you and Raggedy Ann found a cunning little chipmunk baby! And you didn't have spectacles."

"Yes! That is true!" Raggedy Andy agreed. "But you see kind old Doctor Lewellen Stork had the spectacles, and who knows but that he saw the weeny, teeny baby creatures first and then just let Raggedy Ann and me find them to please us?"

"That must have been what he did," Raggedy Ann said. "I remember now that I found the little baby chipmunk just where I had seen kind old Doctor Lewellen Stork looking a moment before! His magic spectacles made the little weeny, teeny chipmunk babies appear so that we could see them."

And as there was nothing else to do, all the woodland creatures went back to the chipmunk home and continued their happiness picnic, and all decided that they would write a nice letter to Doctor Stork and perhaps they too would have as much happiness as the chipmunks with their chipmunk babies.

THE TEENY, WEENY HOUSE

"OH, LOOK, Raggedy Ann!" Raggedy Andy cried as he pointed off through the bushes in the deep, deep woods. "See the little, teeny, weeny path leading under the bushes. Where do you suppose it leads, Raggedy Ann?"

"I don't know, Raggedy Andy," Raggedy Ann replied as she took Raggedy Andy's hand and pulled him under the bushes and down the little teeny, weeny path.

"We will see what is at the end of the path, Raggedy Andy. Maybe it leads to a fairy castle! A little, teeny, weeny fairy castle!"

"Oh, don't you hope it does, Raggedy Ann?" Raggedy Andy said as he followed Raggedy Ann down the little path.

The Raggedys followed the little, teeny, weeny path until they came to a little tinkley brook, and there they found a little, teeny, weeny bridge made of sticks.

"The little, teeny, weeny bridge is too small for us to walk on," Raggedy Ann said. "We would break it down. We must cross on those stepping stones just below."

This the Raggedys did and finally came to the cutest, cunningest little, teeny, weeny house they had ever seen.

"Yes, sir!" said Raggedy Ann. "It must be a fairy's house!"

And as the two Raggedys sat down in front of the little, teeny, weeny house, and admired it, the little, teeny, weeny front door opened and a cunning little lady-creature only two inches high came out to sweep the porch. She wore a tiny lace cap, a flowered dress and a little white apron.

"Why, it is Granny Field-mouse!" Raggedy Ann said.

"Hello, Raggedy Ann and Raggedy Andy!" Granny Field-mouse laughed. "You startled me! I did not know anyone was sitting there."

"When did you move into the deep, deep woods filled with fairies 'n' everything?" Raggedy Ann asked. "You lived in the great yellow meadow when we saw you last." Granny Field-mouse leaned her little broom against the door and sat upon the porch steps.

"I'll tell you all about it, Raggedy Ann and Raggedy Andy," she said. "You remember Granpy and I used to live beside the Looking-glass Brook, in the great yellow meadow, and sometimes when it rained real, real hard the Looking-glass Brook grew so large it came right up and into our house and that wasn't very comfortable.

"One day, Granpy Field-mouse was fishing in the Looking-glass Brook with a broom straw for a pole and a thread for a line, when he heard something go *splash* and there he saw a teeny, weeny little fairy baby in the water.

"Well, Granpy Field-mouse, although he can not swim very well, hopped right in and saved the little, teeny, weeny fairy baby. And when the fairy mama and daddy came running up, they were so glad to find their baby safe and sound, they built us this cunning little, teeny, weeny cottage and ever since then Granpy Field-mouse has worked for the fairies, tending their flower garden. Isn't it nice?"

"Indeed it is, Granny Field-mouse," the Raggedys said. "We wish we could come inside your cunning little, teeny, weeny fairy house, but we are too large!" So Granny

Field-mouse ran into her cunning little house and brought out a lot of field-mouse cookies.

Raggedy Ann and Raggedy Andy lay upon the soft green grass in front of Granny Field-mouse's cunning little cottage. It was the cunningest, cutest little, teeny, weeny house the Raggedys had ever seen, and as they peeped into the windows they nibbled on the lovely field-mouse cookies.

"Can you see the pretty little piano the fairies put in our living room?" Granny Field-mouse asked the Raggedys.

"Is it a real-for-sure piano?" Raggedy Andy asked.

"Oh, indeed it is!" Granny Field-mouse replied. "Just you peep into the window while I run in and tinkle it, Raggedy Ann and Raggedy Andy!" Granny Field-mouse said.

So Granny Field-mouse ran inside her little fairy house and raised the windows, and then she tinkled the cunning little piano.

"It sounds just like a little music box we used to have in the play room," Raggedy Ann told Granny Field-mouse.

"Do you know?" Granny Field-mouse laughed, "Granpy Field-mouse wanted to open it to see where the pretty music comes from, but I said, 'Granpy, don't you dare open the cunning little piano because if you do it may not tinkle any more!' Granpy is just like a great many big boys!" laughed Granny Field-mouse.

Raggedy Ann and Raggedy Andy laughed with Granny Field-mouse for lots and lots of times in the play room at home they had known boys who wanted to pick things to pieces to see where the noise came from.

"You did just right, Granny Field-mouse!" Raggedy Ann said. "And have you a cunning little stove in your kitchen, too?"

"Oh, yes!" Granny Field-mouse replied. "I have to cook Granpy's dinners you know. The fairies did not forget a single thing. Just peep into the bedroom windows, Raggedy Ann and Raggedy Andy, and see the two little, teeny, weeny beds the fairies put in for us!"

And just as the Raggedys were peeping into the little bedroom windows, they heard a racket at the front door.

"Oh, dear!" Granny Field-mouse squeaked as she ran into the kitchen and slammed the door behind her.

"If you don't open the front door, I'll chew a hole in it and gobble you up!" a loud voice called.

The Raggedys looked at each other in surprise, and Raggedy Andy got to his feet softly and tiptoed around the cunning little house. There he saw Walter Weazel starting to chew Granny Field-mouse's nice front door.

Raggedy Andy boxed Walter Weazel's ears as hard as he could with his rag hand, and although Walter Weazel was greatly surprised he jumped upon Raggedy Andy and knocked him over. Then Raggedy Andy rolled up his sleeves, and he and Walter Weazel tussled-and-bustled and wrestled-and-testled until Walter Weazel had torn a great many holes in Raggedy Andy's pretty blue and red striped shirt. This was too much for Granny Field-mouse. She ran out of her little kitchen and whacked Walter Weazel right upon the nose with her broom handle.

Then, when Walter Weazel had run howling away, Granny Field-mouse sewed up all the holes in Raggedy Andy's shirt and gave him a lot more field-mouse cookies.

"Wasn't it rude of Walter Weazel to come right up on your front porch and start chewing your front door, Granny Field-mouse?" Raggedy Andy said after Granny Field-mouse had mended the holes.

"Indeed it was!" Granny Fieldmouse replied. "And I am not a bit sorry that I whacked Walter Weazel on the nose with my broom handle! Not even a teeny, weeny speck!"

"I hope he never comes back to chew your front door again," said Raggedy Ann.

"So do I!" Granny Field-mouse answered. "It isn't very pleasant to have anyone frighten you!"

"Indeed it isn't!" Raggedy Andy agreed.

After they had finished eating the field-mouse cookies and had visited a while, Raggedy Ann and Raggedy Andy started on their way again. They had not gone far when they heard some one running through the deep, deep woods as fast as he could come, and there was a great deal of squealing and squeaking, too.

"Mercy!" cried Raggedy Ann. "Do you think Walter Weazel has come back to bother Granny Field-mouse, Raggedy Andy?"

Raggedy Andy picked up a stick and ran back to Granny Field-mouse's cunning little teeny, weeny cottage.

"Ha!" said Raggedy Andy. "Just see, Raggedy Ann!"

There came Granpy Field-mouse, running as hard as his little legs would carry him, while close behind him came Walter Weazel and his daddy. Granpy had barely time to jump inside the front door and slam it behind him when the Weazels were on the front porch.

"You mean little Field-mice!" Walter Weazel's daddy squealed. "What do you mean by hurting my poor little Weazel-boy?"

"I did not hurt him!" Granpy Field-mouse cried from inside his house.

"Well, Granny Field-mouse whacked him on the nose with her broom handle," squealed Walter Weazel's daddy.

"That was because he started chewing our front door," Granny Field-mouse replied.

"Well," said Walter Weazel's daddy, "Walter Weazel has a perfect right to eat Field-mice whenever he catches them, so, because you were mean to Walter Weazel, we will both chew a hole in your front door and eat you up!"

Walter Weazel and his daddy both started chewing the Field-mouse's front door, but before they could make more than a scratch, Raggedy Ann and Raggedy Andy ran up, each with big sticks and whacked the wicked Weazels so hard and fast the Weazels squealed and squawked.

"There!" cried Raggedy Ann and Raggedy Andy as

Walter Weazel and his daddy ran away, holding their heads. "You'll remember what you got this time, and if we ever find you bothering the Field-mice again, we will treat you worse than we did this time."

And Walter Weazel and his daddy ran home and told Mama Weazel.

"Mama Weazel," they said, "do not ever go to Granny Field-mouse's and try to chew the doors, for you will get so many whacks with big sticks you will be sorry for a long, long time."

And as Mama Weazel wrapped up their heads in vinegar and brown paper, she thought to herself, "You bet I won't and you won't either!"

And after that the Weazels never came near the cunning little home of the Field-mice again.

THE LAST STORY OF ALL

THE FAIRY WISH

AFTER leaving the Field-mouse home the Raggedys walked through the deep, deep woods and came to a whole lot of mushrooms. The mushrooms grew side by side, and they formed a large ring.

"Here is a Fairy Ring!" said Raggedy Andy. "Let's sit here, and perhaps the fairies will come and dance."

"It would be lovely to watch the pretty little fairies come here and dance," Raggedy Ann replied as she sat down upon the soft moss.

The Raggedys sat near the Fairy Ring for a long, long time but they did not get fidgety. No, sir! The Raggedys knew that if they waited long enough they would see the pretty little fairies come to the Fairy Ring to have a dance. And sure enough, pretty soon, after the long, long time of waiting, one little fairy came and sat upon a mushroom, then another and another fairy flew up and sat upon a mushroom until every mushroom had a fairy seated upon it.

"Aren't they just the sweetest little creatures you ever saw?" Raggedy Andy whispered.

Raggedy Ann could only wag her doll head, "Yes!" for her shoe button eyes had never seen lovelier little creatures.

Presently the Fairy Queen flew down into the center of the Fairy Ring and waved her tiny wand. All the fairies jumped from the mushrooms and circled about her.

The Raggedys held their rag-breaths until the fairy dance was over. Then the Fairy Queen laughed and asked, "Why are you sitting there watching us, Raggedy Ann and Raggedy Andy?"

"Because you are the prettiest, dearest, little fairies we have ever seen," Raggedy Ann replied.

"Thank you!" all the cunning little fairies laughed.

"Now," the Fairy Queen said to Raggedy Ann and Raggedy Andy, "maybe you do not know it, but we watched you take care of Granny and Granpy Field-mouse and their house, and we will let you make one wish, and have the wish come true!"

"Thank you, Fairy Queen!" the Raggedys said.

Then they thought and thought and whispered together. Finally Raggedy Andy said, "Raggedy Ann has thought of a good wish."

"That is nice!" the Fairy Queen laughed. "What is it, Raggedy Ann?"

"I wish that all around the cunning little teeny, weeny house of Granny and Granpy Field-mouse there was an invisible wall so that only those who are friends of Granny and Granpy could visit them!"

"That is a nice, nice wish," the Fairy Queen said. "And the nicest part is that it is an unselfish wish. Your wish shall come true, Raggedy Ann and Raggedy Andy. And maybe you do not know it," the Fairy Queen continued, "but almost every unselfish wish in the world comes true, whether there are fairies about, or not!"

Look for these other Raggedy Ann Books